THE BRONZE MIRROR

Book One of
SPIRALS OF TIME

Margaret Iggulden

THREE OAK LEAVES PRESS

First edition published in 2022 by Three Oak Leaves Press.

Print ISBN 978-1-7397839-0-7

Ebook ISBN 978-1-7397839-1-4

Cover artwork by Angela Davis

Cover design by Clarkes Printing, Monmouth

For my mother, Kathleen

& my grandmother, Elizabeth

The Bronze Mirror

CONTENTS

Prologue

'You will be reborn on a planet,' the Goddess said. 'When you are twelve, you will remember this quest.'

The girl and the boy – twins – stood in front of the Goddess. Dazzling bright lights shone from her head. Blue, red, green, yellow, orange, in all their different shades, making a huge rainbow around her.

They had been summoned to the Planet Kircus, deep, deep in the far Universe. They shivered. It was always cold on this star.

'We have chosen your family, and where you shall live, so that you may fulfil a quest. This must be completed before the end of this era.'

The twins listened. For all their other lives, they had chosen their parents, and where they would live: the deserts of Neptune, the oceans of Jupiter, the cold wastes of Saturn. Now, they were being sent away once more. Why? What was so different about this life?

They stood, waiting for the Goddess to speak again.

'You must complete the first task. Then, and only then, you will be led to the second. Watch and listen. Stay on the path. For you have much to do. Great perils await you.' The Goddess paused. 'On this planet, many things need changing. When you have completed one task, you must cast a crystal into water. That crystal will cleanse the rivers, the seas, the oceans.'

From the hands of the Goddess, crystals floated: rose, purple, dark green, pure white, and swirls of amber. Glowing, shimmering, reflecting the brightness all around them, they attached themselves to the twins.

'If you follow the path, if you fulfil the quest, you will save this planet.'

The twins saw a beautiful blue orb moving in the Heavens from east to west, half in light and half in darkness; a sun, and a moon. Stars flickered like jewels around, above and beyond this planet.

The twins smiled. This had been their home before.

'You know this planet well. That is why you have been chosen. Your actions will save it from darkest night, from extinction.'

The planet came into sharper focus. Grey skies, burnt trees, dirty rivers, cities choking. Thousands of years had passed since they had lived there. They remembered it as pure, pristine. The twins felt sadness as they pictured the blue oceans, snow-capped mountains: people and trees, insects and animals, all living together in harmony. The images faded, and disappeared.

'Do you accept this quest? Will you return to Planet Earth for one more lifetime?'

'Yes, we will.'

Lights from the Goddess surrounded the girl and boy.

'We will send others at different times to help you with this quest. Take notice of those who will try to stop you. They will try to thwart you: one of you, or both. Be aware. Stay on the path and you will succeed. Stray off the path and you will fail, then Life on this planet will die.'

The twins felt the power of the crystals all around them, protecting them for the tasks ahead.

'All is ready.' There was a pause in time. 'I will now breathe you into existence,' said the Goddess.

The twins felt themselves floating down, down, through the dark mass, enveloped by the dust of the Universe.

Chapter 1
The Quest Begins

As they drove through the steep-sided valley, Tara was looking up at the white, craggy cliffs. She brushed her fringe out of her eyes to see more clearly; waves of trees stretched far above, up to the skyline. Leaves shimmered in the summer sun; light green, dark green.

'Wow, what awesome ruins!' said her twin brother, David. 'Can we stop?'

'Where? What ruins?' asked Tara.

'That's Tintern Abbey,' said their mother, Suzi. 'Isn't it stunning? I'll drive past slowly, so you can get a good look.'

Tara turned and, as she did, she saw a huge grey stone building with towering walls and pillars. Sunlight glinted on the stained glass in the massive arched window. Blues, reds, greens, yellows. It looked amazing.

'Yes, the colours are beautiful,' she said. 'Who are those men in the long white and black clothes, walking around? Are they singing?'

'What colours? I didn't see any men,' said David. 'You must be imagining things again.' He sighed and stroked Bethan, their new puppy, who was sleeping between them on the back seat.

Tara swallowed. This kept happening. As they had crossed the bridge into Wales, she had seen lines of men dressed as Roman soldiers marching.

'Is there a re-enactment around here today?' she'd asked her parents. She was puzzled, as the men looked as if they were walking a metre above the ground, but she'd decided not to mention that part. Perhaps it was something to do with moving from London to the Wye Valley. Perhaps she was just excited about their new life. Strange that no one else was seeing these things, though.

'You'll have plenty of time to explore all around here during the holidays,' said Suzi. 'We need to get to our new home and unpack. We'll be living in the main house; the guest house is separate.'

'We must think of a new name for it,' said Ben.

'I should think so, Dad,' said David. '*Wyeland* isn't exactly cool, is it?'

'Think of something zippy then,' said his father.

'Zippy?' came a murmur from the back seat.

'Ah, Simone – are you tired after your early start? You left Rome at dawn, and it's nearly six o'clock now.'

'*Si.* I mean "yes"! But I'm fine, Aunt Suzi. Really. Mamma said we'll be going to a dig. What's a dig?

A concert?'

David began explaining to his cousin about discovering gold coins and swords.

Simone frowned at him. 'You have swords in your garden?'

'David, go easy on your cousin today. Remember she hasn't been speaking English for a few months. Speak slower!' said Suzi, as she waited behind a large group of cyclists.

'Just saying. Anyway, I'm sure we'll find all kinds of ancient things. I mean to have a museum in one of the sheds. Skulls, bones.'

'Remember to wear a pirate's hat!' Tara grinned.

'You've got a day at Trellech at the dig, tomorrow,' said Ben, 'and your mum and I thought you'd enjoy cycling up there.'

He waved his hand in the direction of a narrow road, which rose up steeply and disappeared into woods.

'That's the Angidy Valley. You'll go past an old lime kiln. It's way up there, at the top of that hill.'

'You are making a... a joke,' Simone laughed.

'Joke? Actually, no!' said Ben. 'We have to get the house ready, as guests will be arriving in a few days' time.'

Simone looked moodily at the river as they waited for the traffic lights to change. She watched a heron on the riverbank, standing still, staring into the waters. Slowly, he lifted his long legs and flew off down the river. *I wish I could go with him.*

'So,' said Ben, 'we thought you'd enjoy one day at the dig, looking for treasure.'

'Treasure,' muttered Simone to herself, rolling her eyes.

'There are some mysterious standing stones near it.' Suzi drove around a fallen branch on the road. 'You might discover something – like pottery.'

'Pottery!' said David. 'What about gold and silver coins? You hear about amazing hoards like Sutton Ho. Then we can be rich, and not have any guests.'

His parents looked at one another and smiled.

'Rich or poor; it doesn't make any difference. This is our dream,' said Suzi.

Several canoes were on the river. In one was a small brown dog, tail up, watching the churning waters. A young girl in a helmet and an orange suit was paddling through the rapids. Some small children were laughing and pointing at nearby rocks.

'That looks great!' said Tara. 'Doesn't it, Simone?'

'Hmm–'

'It's the perfect place for us all, and people can come for activity holidays; painting, photography, walking Offa's Dyke...' said Ben.

'Exploring!' David moved Bethan onto his lap. She opened her mouth, yawned widely, and went back to sleep.

'Will you get ponies?' asked Simone.

'Yes, we hope so. And we'll grow vegetables, have beehives, chickens...'

'And will you go – shipping soon?'

'Shopping? I hope not!' David was watching two swans glide along the river.

Simone ignored him. 'Isn't your house too near the water, though? Mamma said something about lots of rain and – fl-flooding–?'

'No, it's never flooded,' said her uncle. 'I don't know where she got that idea from!'

David looked at Simone, put his thumb and forefinger together, and made a motion over his lips. 'Zip,' he whispered.

'Zippy?' She looked confused.

'Shush. Sore point,' said Tara, shaking her head. 'Are we there yet, Mum?'

'Yes! This is it! Your new home. What do you think?' Suzi swung the car into the drive.

In front of them was a large white house, with red roses climbing all over the front porch. "1639" was carved into the stone at the top of the gable. A steep track led up to the woods behind, and at the end of a path there were some old wooden sheds covered in brambles. Away from the house and its huge garden was a small cottage with a fence around it.

The twins and their brown-and-white spaniel tumbled out of the car.

'Love it,' said Tara, looking around as two butterflies sped by and vanished up into the woodland.

'Awesome!' David shouted as he raced down the

path towards the sheds. Bethan ran after him and started spinning around in circles.

'Lots of space for a trench. I can dig for–'

'For potatoes,' called Suzi after him. 'Bethan can help you!'

'During the holidays we really have to start puppy training!' said Ben as he turned the key in the door.

'That'll be fun! Where is she?'

Suzi turned around. The spaniel had stopped dead in the drive. Then she began barking at the empty house.

'Bethan! Stop!'

'Maybe she can sense something, Mum.' Tara stared up. She could see there had been two houses, now they were joined together. As she glanced along them, a shape flittered across the window at the end.

'She probably wants her dinner,' said Ben, opening the door wide and stepping into the hallway. There was a corridor to the left, and one to the right with a door marked "Private". A wooden staircase led up to the first floor.

'Well, she'll have to wait until we've eaten – new rules.' Suzi bent down to stroke the excited puppy. 'New rules, Bethan.'

'Was that a neighbour in the house, Dad?' Tara carried her backpack to the bottom of the stairs.

'Where? No. There's no one here, or living near here. Helen and Mike are our closest neighbours, and they live about a quarter of a mile away, towards Redbrook.'

David raced inside. 'There are lots of shelves in those sheds. Great for my collection!' He ran up the stairs two at a time. 'It's really cool here.'

'We can get honey and eggs from the neighbours, too, until we have our own bees and chickens,' said Suzi. 'Right, let's put the boxes of food in the kitchen.'

David hung over the banister. 'Hurry up! I've chosen my bedroom already!'

'No, you haven't. I'm having the one overlooking the river.' Tara picked up her backpack, and bumped it up the stairs.

'What did I–?' Ben called. 'Oh – never mind.' He turned into the kitchen, with the puppy on his heels. 'I'd better put her bedding down. Then she'll get used to her own space.'

'I think our niece is feeling a bit homesick. Can you see what she's doing?'

Simone was sitting on a garden bench, looking at the view. Across the river, sheep were grazing in the fields. 'It's tranquil. Very quiet here.'

'It certainly is,' said her uncle. 'Very different from Rome. But there's plenty of water!'

He pointed to a tiny stream trickling down over mossy stones and overhung by ferns. 'That's the water for our house.'

Horrified, Simone jumped up to look at it. 'Is it clean? Will I get ill?'

Ben laughed. 'No! Don't worry. It's fine. We collect rainwater in those barrels, for showers and the loo.'

The young girl stared at her uncle and twisted the end of her long black plait; she was confused and worried.

'Enough, Ben. Stop teasing her!' Suzi called as she came out to pick up more boxes.

'Oh, OK! We are on mains water. There's a reservoir way up there above us. I've been told the water even tastes quite good!'

'Stop it! David must get his joking habit from you!' Suzi hugged her niece. 'It's going to be great having you here for the summer.'

Simone looked away, and swallowed hard. She had wanted to spend the holidays at home, but her parents were busy working, and it was too hot to stay with her other cousins in Egypt.

'Now, your bedroom is next to Tara's. There's a connecting door, so you two can chat all night if you want to! Supper will be in an hour.' Suzi looked into a pair of watery dark eyes. 'We're all going to have a great time.'

Simone nodded. '*Si.* OK, Aunt Suzi.'

A flash of brown and white ran past them and up the stairs as they walked back into the hallway.

'Bethan! No!' called Ben. 'Can someone bring her down?'

'Come on up, Simone!' Tara called. 'Your bedroom is really cool. It's got a view of the woods.'

She stopped. 'Have you been cooking already, Dad? I can smell bread... or maybe pastry? Are we having quiche?'

Everyone sniffed. 'I can't smell nothing,' said Simone.

'Anything,' David jumped down the stairs two at a time and ran along the corridor towards the kitchen.

'You can't smell anything, neither?' asked Simone.

He turned and opened his mouth.

'David!' said his mother. 'Stop correcting her all the time. In the end, she'll clam up. Let her be.'

She walked down to the sitting room and sniffed. 'I can't smell anything cooking. The oven hasn't been used for over a month. They left it all spotless.'

'I'm going to make lentil bake,' said Ben.

Simone picked up her backpack and slowly, miserably, went upstairs. 'Lentil bake,' she muttered under her breath.

They sat around the large pine table in the kitchen to eat supper. The shelves were already full of mugs and plates, glasses and jugs.

Suzi had fixed a baby gate across the entrance to the utility room. Bethan was behind it, peeking through the slats.

'You've a cosy bed and your own space, little puppy,' she said. 'Be happy!'

The spaniel stared up at her with large brown eyes, and whined softly.

'Oh cool, Dad. Lentil bake and mushrooms,' said David. 'My favourite.'

Simone was pushing the brown mixture around her plate.

'So, let's have a think about a new name for this place,' said Ben. 'It's a guest house, not just a B&B. And there's the cottage for guests who want to cook for themselves.'

'Oh, is there?' asked Simone. 'Could Tara and I stay there for the holidays? I could cook pizza and lasagne. Dad taught me how to make Egyptian chicken – er – things.'

Suzi looked over at Ben. 'I don't think our niece is too keen on lentils.'

'Bethan can eat hers.' David leant over to take the plate.

'No, she can't. She has dried dog food and leftover vegetables,' said his mother.

'I'll rustle you up a cheese and tomato omelette,' said Ben. 'No problem.'

Simone gave her uncle a grateful smile as he reached for a knife and started chopping up some tomatoes. 'Now, come on. Think of some names instead of *Wyeland*.'

'The Snowy Owl,' suggested Tara. She was staring out of the window at an old lady who was throwing something from a wicker basket. The woman was wearing a long brown dress with a black shawl. 'Who–?' She stopped. Every time she asked if they could see someone or something, they couldn't. *I'd better not say anything,* she thought. *It's only been since... Oh, it's been happening since we visited Avebury and I leant against the standing stones there. I expect it'll all just go away.*

'Snowy Owl,' said Suzi. 'That sounds a bit too cold. Help yourself to salad, everyone.'

'The Black Cat,' said David. 'They are lucky.'

'In Italy, they are bad luck,' said Simone, turning over the lettuce with her fork.

'Are you checking for slu–?'

Tara sent her twin The Look.

'How about The Barnacled Goose?' said Ben swirling the eggs around the pan.

'Not cool,' said David. 'Definitely not cool, Dad.'

'The Seven Magpies,' said his twin, as she counted the birds strutting and pecking at the front lawn. *Seven for a secret never to be told,* she thought. *I wonder what the secret will be?*

'How about The Scraggy Chicken... The Hot Goat... The–?'

'Very funny, David,' said his mother. 'We'll sleep on it, and maybe we'll decide later this week. It needs to reflect the spirit of this valley, and catch the imagination...'

'Right, Mum. We get it.' David was measuring out Bethan's dinner into her bowl.

The puppy sat expectantly behind the slats of the

baby gate, following his every movement.

David leaned over, held the food up, counted to five, and then put it down on the floor. Bethan scoffed it within a minute. 'Good girl!'

Everyone laughed, even Simone.

David turned around to look at his family. 'What? I read about how to train a puppy on a website.'

'Are you sure it wasn't a–' began Tara.

'–wolf!' said Simone.

'Bravo!' said Suzi.

David grinned.

'Oh I forgot,' said Ben. 'Your bikes are ready to go.'

Simone looked shocked. 'I haven't ridden one for a long time.'

'You'll be fine. I think Rhys and Isabelle from the farmhouse opposite are going to the dig, too. You'll like them. They are about your age,' said Suzi.

'Can we take Bethan, Mum?'

'Sure. Tara, your bike has a basket on the front if she gets tired.'

'And I'll make packed lunches,' added Ben.

'What do archeys eat?' asked David.

'Archeys?' Tara was staring out of the window. 'Architects?'

A man on horseback was galloping past. He was wearing a large hat with a feather. But was he really there? She looked again. No. There was no man; just a breeze blowing the branches of the birch trees.

'Archaeologists. Diggers,' said David as he squeezed a rubber ball, ready to play catch with the puppy.

'There were a few caravans there. Perhaps they'll cook something in their own kitchens.'

'Aunt Suzi, we do – we have – a lot of ruins and – and – old things in Italy,' said Simone. 'Could I stay here tomorrow? I feel I need to rest.'

'You can chat to everyone there, and improve your English. It will be lovely,' said her aunt briskly. 'You'll have great memories of your summer holidays, and be able to tell all your friends when you get back to school.'

Simone sighed deeply. 'And my phone–?'

Suzi and Ben exchanged glances.

'Ah. There's no cover in this area at all.'

'No signal.'

'We're living in the Dark Ages!' said David.

'You must have been a queen, or a lady of the court in a past life,' said Tara quietly. 'Or maybe you were... a king...'

Everyone stared at her. 'Joke. Joke.'

'It is difficult for me. It is, really.' Simone's eyes welled up.

'Bed now!' said Suzi. 'You're all very tired.'

'I'll take Bethan for a quick walk around the garden,' said Ben. 'She never gets tired!'

Lying in bed, Tara could hear her parents discussing where to put up their paintings in the sitting room. Simone was unpacking in the next room. Something crashed.

'Are you alright?'

'*Si. Si.* Yes. I think so. Are you glad you've moved here, Tara?'

'Oh, yes. I prefer being in the countryside. Come in, sit on my bed.'

She patted the blue-and-white duvet cover. 'It's been ages since we last saw you. But we're going to have a brilliant time this holidays. It'll be fun.'

Simone nodded. 'I hope so.'

'And we can visit some caves—'

'Caves?' Simone gasped.

'There are loads of castles around here, too. And Nanny Lita and Grandpa want us to stay with them for a few days. We can visit Caerleon.'

Simone smiled. '*Bene.* Good. That will be nice.'

'There's the Forest of Dean, too. We could walk—'

'Can we go to London? I'd like to go on the round thing—'

'The Eye!' Tara exclaimed. 'We've just come from there, so we thought you'd like to explore the valley with us. Maybe we can have a day in a city somewhere later. Cardiff is great. It's got museums.'

'Shops, too?'

'Sleep!' called Suzi. 'Busy day tomorrow!'

Tara woke up. How long had she been asleep? There was a slight rushing sound. Was it the wind in the trees? She glanced out of the window and saw the sky; dark, yet full of stars. The moon was almost completely round. Was it a new moon or a full moon, she wondered. A figure moved across the bottom of her bed. 'Mum?' she whispered. It continued to move, and then disappeared into the wall. *What is happening? Why can I see people who are not there?* Questions filled her head until she drifted off into dreams of small, round boats whirling towards a night-black entrance.

Chapter 2
At the Dig

'Our neighbours were telling us that this house is haunted!' said Ben, laughing as the children drifted down to breakfast.

'Great!' said David. 'Spooky! There'll be vampires in the sheds!'

'Hunted?' asked Simone as she stared at the bowl of creamy porridge in front of her and reached for the toast instead.

'Haunted,' Tara said quickly, as she saw her brother about to open his mouth.

'Ghosts. Spirits. People who are dead.'

'Oh, we have plenty in our house. They throw things and walk along – walk through walls. It's normal.' Simone buttered her toast.

The family looked at her, and burst out laughing.

'What? What now?' she asked.

'We're not laughing at you. It's just, well–' said her aunt.

'We are surprised, that's all. We never had anything like that in our last home.' Ben handed out the packed lunches. 'Any home, come to think of it.'

'Cosmic! Can we come and stay with you in our next holidays?' asked David.

'Of course. There's a man with his head underneath his elbow... er–'

There was silence. 'Shoulder... ah – arm.'

David stared at her.

'Now I'm teasing you!' grinned his cousin.

'Upstairs and get ready!' said Suzi. 'No, not you, Bethan. Sit.'

Tara pulled on the jeans and t-shirt she'd worn yesterday. Socks? She found two at the bottom of her backpack. One red, one yellow.

'What are you wearing, Simone? Have you got some old things to throw on?'

She looked around the door. Her cousin was brushing her long dark hair in front of a mirror.

'Are we the same height now?'

Tara stood next to her. 'No, you're still taller than me. I can't see that ever changing!'

With large dark eyes and olive skin, her cousin looked more like her Egyptian family.

'David and I take after the other side of our family. Me – shorter, a bit rounder, like Mum. For twins, we're an interesting mixture.' She touched her straight, light red-brown hair. 'This could be the Celtic bit from Mum, or Dad – he is convinced he's Viking! Not sure where these green eyes came from!' She stared into the mirror.

'And from Grandma Lita, we have her Welsh-Caribbean in us, too.'

'We're just awesome!' Tara hugged her cousin as they smiled at each other's reflections. 'Let's ask if we can have our DNAs done this holiday. That would be fun.'

'Perhaps we'll find out that we are from different planets!'

'David sure is!'

They both laughed.

Simone finished plaiting her hair, and looked under the bed for her trainers.

'Tara, you've got odd socks on!'

'Can't find a pair. It doesn't matter. They feel the same.'

The girl from Rome sighed and adjusted her sunglasses. She checked in the mirror. Long white shirt, light blue jeans, a matching cotton sweater. Plait on the left. She was ready for the day.

David put his head around the door. He gasped. 'You're not going dressed like that?'

'*Si*. Yes. Why not?'

'It's a dig. Dirt. Mud. Earth.'

She shrugged. 'You can dig. I won't!'

'Come on, or you'll be late,' called Ben. 'Your lunch boxes are on the kitchen table.'

They ran downstairs and put the drinks and sandwiches into their backpacks.

'Now Tara, you've got the directions. I did give them to you, didn't I?'

'Yes, Mum.' Tara tapped the back pocket of her jeans. 'It's down the path here, and onto the road to the Abbey. Go along for about five minutes, then turn right up the hill. Keep going straight up, until we get to the top. There's a crossroads, and we turn right towards Trellech, whiz along, past the field with the standing stones. Then turn left, and the dig is on the right.'

'Are there toilets there?' asked Simone anxiously.

'I think we saw a couple of those mobile blue loos, didn't we, Ben?'

'There's always the fields,' said David, as he took the puppy's leash from the hook. 'Come on, Bethan.'

'Remember to clean up after her,' called Suzi. 'Take some of those bags. And don't hang them on the trees.'

Simone closed her eyes. *My British family are quite strange.*

'Mum, what did the neighbours say about the hauntings?' asked Tara.

Suzi was giving her niece another hug, and hoping that she would settle in. 'Eight weeks here when you are twelve years old must feel like a lifetime,' she had said to Ben earlier. 'She did seem brighter this morning, though.'

'Mum?'

'There's an old woman who wears a shawl and goes out with her basket to feed her chickens. She lived here in the 1800s, apparently. She sometimes wanders around at night. But she's quite harmless. She baked for the people in the area, so at different times of the year you'd smell her cooking; Welsh cakes, bara brith.'

'We can call her Mrs Baker,' said Simone.

Tara laughed. 'Brilliant, cuz!' She was relieved that she wasn't the only one who had seen her.

'Why–?' David began as he strolled back into the kitchen.

'Get your skates on. The archaeologists won't wait for you!' said Ben. 'It's 8.30 already. We'll see you about five or six o'clock tonight.'

'Have a good day!' called Suzi as they waved them off.

The children were pushing their bikes slowly up the steep hill. Simone had taken off her sweater, and was breathing hard as she pushed her bike around a corner.

'Where…? How…?' she panted. '*No. No…*'

'It can't be that far now,' said Tara, trying to sound cheerful.

As they came around a bend, they saw Bethan wagging her tail at a grey-haired woman, who was cutting some roses in her garden.

'Lovely day for a bike ride,' the woman called over to them.

David pointed to the name on the wooden gate – Awkward Hill House – and laughed. 'That's a funny name. It's perfect!'

The children stopped pushing their bikes. 'How far is it to Trellech?' asked Tara. 'We're going to the dig, and we're puffed out already.'

'Good for you! Cyclists and archaeologists!' said the woman. 'We get lots around here.' She took off her gardening gloves and wiped her forehead. 'There are another three bends, and then you come to the crossroads. It's quite flat after that. Go past the field with the standing stones, and turn right.'

Simone sighed. '*Bene.* Oh good.'

'Just think, when you've finished today, you can come down on your bikes like a helter-skelter!' laughed the woman.

'Hell–?

'So not far now. Bye!' said Tara. 'And thank you!'

The puppy had dived across the road, to a stream that was trickling down by the side. She lapped thirstily at the water, then crashed into the woods.

'Bethan, come back!' called Tara. 'Go after her, David. She's more your dog than–'

'No, she's *our* dog.'

'Well, you are the one she listens to, and it's your job to train her,' snapped Tara.

Her cousin looked at her, surprised.

'Sorry, just a bit hot and tired, and I didn't sleep

very well last night.' Tara breathed in and out very slowly.

'Wow! There's a kind of small building over there, covered with ivy and stuff. Some black bits are on the ground, maybe charcoal,' called David. 'Hey–'

'*Andiamo!* Let's go!' shouted Simone, as she put her head down, and began pushing the bike up the hill with great determination. 'Nearly there...'

Tara wondered if their parents had realised how steep this valley was.

'It's like training for a marathon,' she panted, remembering the day her mum ran one in London. 'Maybe we could all run a half-marathon next year.'

'And take Bethan with us,' said David as he put her in Tara's basket. The puppy licked Tara's hand, and stared deeply into her eyes.

'Thanks, Twin. You've just made my job even harder! Yes, I love you, Bethan. But stop licking my fingers!' She heaved a sigh. 'Let's take five!'

The three turned and looked back. Down in the valley, wisps of mist were drifting up, trailing past the dense woodland that stretched along the skyline. Below them, the river flowed on, then vanished around a bend, towards Tintern, on to Chepstow, and out into the sea.

'I wonder if there are hidden gorges over there?' said David.

'Enchanted valleys,' said Simone.

'Deep, secret caves,' added Tara. 'Come on! Let's go!'

A church clock was chiming as the three children cycled past the standing stones, and turned right up towards the dig. Throwing their bikes into the nearest hedge, they ran to join the group of people sitting on the grass. Bethan wagged her tail, and strained at her leash.

'Shush. Sit.' David held her tightly. 'Now, behave.'

Tara looked around. It was a huge, flat field, with lumps and bumps all over it. Moles? she wondered. At one end was a large white tent with long tables. Small caravans were dotted around the site, away from a few long ditches. Mounds of earth were piled up next to them; the remains of ancient walls could be seen.

She sat on the edge of the group of volunteers behind David. Bethan was squirming on her leash, eager to meet everyone.

'Sit. There's a good girl.'

Two women and two men were standing in front of the group, examining a large map on a whiteboard. All were wearing blue helmets, thick socks, boots, t-shirts, and jeans.

'Do we have to wear those terrible hats?' asked Simone, as she placed a cloth carefully on the grass and sat on it. 'I don't like wearing these things on my head.' She took off her cycling helmet, and rearranged her plait.

'I don't know.' Tara smiled at her cousin. "Our drama queen", as she and David called her.

She pushed her hair behind her ears. 'Maybe we should've got our hair cut very short for the holidays! Then this might grow back curly – like David's.'

'*No! No!*' shrieked Simone.

As they burst out laughing, the puppy jumped up, barked loudly, and ran in a circle around David.

'You've tied me up with your leash, Bethan!'

'Whose dog is that?' shouted a tall man with a grey beard.

'She's ours,' called Tara, wondering why he'd asked. Obviously, the spaniel was theirs. 'She's fine.'

'Dogs always get in the way.' He turned to a short, stocky woman, who was frowning and staring at a clipboard. 'I thought you'd banned them, Tabitha,' he said crossly.

'I did, Paul. I did.'

He turned to David. 'You'll have to tie it up till we have a break.'

'She's a puppy–' David began angrily as he untangled the leash.

'Just tie it up by the fence over there, and take it for a very long walk at lunchtime.'

'Let her sit next to the lad as he's digging.' The tall, thin woman smiled at the spaniel. 'I'm sure she'll be alright.'

'You always say that about everything, Ruth.'

A boy with sticking-out ears, sitting near the trio, started sniggering. 'Fancy bringing a dog on a dig. How st–'

Simone glared at him. She curled her lip, looked him up and down, shrugged, and turned away.

Tara tried not to laugh as the boy flushed a deep red. Perhaps she was right, and her cousin really had been a queen in a previous life!

'Listen up, everyone.' The short, stocky woman began. 'My name's Tabitha, and this is Ruth, Paul and Alan.' She waved her hand towards the other three adults. 'As you can see, there are four trenches here. You'll be put into groups. Some of you will have a trowel. Uncover the soil gently, remember! Others will be putting the soil in those buckets there, and some will be using the sieves. Yesterday, we had a very exciting find – an axe.' She glanced around the group. 'Well done, Toby.'

The boy with the sticking-out ears smirked.

'We'll be dating it soon. Last week, we unearthed quite a lot of early medieval pottery, so it's taking some days to date it all. Over to you, Paul.'

Scowling, the man glanced down at his notes.

'He looks like a bull,' whispered David. 'Look, ears back, chin stuck out, and – watch out! He's about to charge!'

Tara pressed her hand over her mouth. Simone asked quietly, 'Why are you laughing?'

'Tell you later,' said Tara, biting her lip.

'It could be that Romans were based here, and so we'll be digging another trench at the far end of the field later,' said Paul. 'The spades are over there.'

'Couldn't you send up a plane with a laser gadget to take pictures, or a drone? Or walk up and down a field with a – a – thingy? Two sticks going down, and one across. Then you can see what's under the ground.'

'Do a geophys survey, you mean?' said Ruth.

'Or you could get a digger in,' added David.

There was a long silence.

'Haven't you got any metal detectors? I saw all those programmes on TV. It'd be a lot quicker.'

The silence deepened. Tara kicked her brother gently in the back.

Tabitha took off her helmet, and ran her fingers through her short, dark hair.

'Thank you for sharing, young man.' She pulled her lips into a tight smile. The shape came, it went. 'And your name is–?'

'David.' He smiled at her. 'And this is my twin sister, Tara, and our cousin, just over from Rome, Simone De Luca Sedky. She's quite bored with ruins, really. They've got so many amazing ones over there, haven't they?'

Everyone turned to stare at Simone. She realised that her cousin had annoyed the team, although didn't quite understand why. Some of the teenagers were grinning.

'Time to go into your different groups,' Tabitha announced as she checked her watch and looked at her clipboard. She gave the trio an irritated look.

'I'll separate you three. It might work then. Toby, you can have – David - in your group.'

The volunteers spent the morning digging, carrying buckets, and trying to avoid the large molehills. Tara had been given a trowel, and was gently removing soil from the bottom of the first trench. Wiping her forehead, she reached for a bottle of water. She wondered how Simone was getting on. She saw her talking to Tabitha by the second trench.

'*Per favore.* Please. Can I ask you some questions? When I get back to school, I will write a report – for our school magazine. Diplomats and, er, presidents' children go to my school. This dig – it will be famous in Roma, in all Italy!'

Tabitha switched on a smile, 'Of course, of course. Ask away.'

'*Grazie.* Thank you.' Simone smiled and took out a pen and a notebook from her backpack. 'What is the best thing you – ever found?'

'Well, it was a gold brooch, and so rare.'

'Rare?' Simone put on a puzzled look. She was determined to keep the woman talking. *Then I won't have to do any digging*, she thought. *Getting my hands dirty isn't my idea of fun.*

Tara smiled. What a clever cousin she had!

'Unique. A unique gold brooch. It was from the ninth century, and it's in the National Museum in Cardiff now,' said Tabitha, putting her shoulders back, and puffing herself up.

Simone nodded as she scribbled on her notepad. '*Magnifico!*'

'Never mix up treasure-hunting with archaeology,' said Paul, as he strolled over to the furthest trench.

'*No, no.* Of course not. This is so, er, awesome.'

Tabitha frowned. 'Remember, anything you find. Anything. Bring it to me.'

'To us,' Alan called over. He was examining a piece of pottery. 'Might be early medieval.'

'Yes, yes. Everything has to go into the tent to be dated.'

Tara took another gulp of water, and saw her brother digging in the new trench. He looked absorbed. 'I'd like to have a collection of things, of finds, in a shed in our garden,' he was saying. 'Like a museum. It'd be amazing. There could be a shelf for Romans, another for Anglo Saxons – and whoever comes after them. Er–'

'Don't you know?' asked Toby, as he sieved some

soil. 'You are st–'

'Call me stupid one more time and I'll–' flashed David, turning towards him.

'You'll what?' Toby dropped the sieve and stood over him.

David jumped up. He was shorter than the boy, but stared straight into his eyes. He wasn't afraid of him. 'Back off–'

Bethan growled, and bared her teeth.

An older teenager stepped between the boys. 'Hey, guys. Just cool it. OK? Come and help me dig over this area. David, is it?'

'Yes.' David exchanged furious looks with Toby, tightened the puppy's leash, and followed the boy to a trench near the white tent.

'I'm Rhys, by the way. What you were saying, about putting things you find in your shed? That's great. But you can't take anything from here, not from this field.' He picked up a trowel, and started to scrape away at the top layer of soil. 'It belongs to the owner of the land; in this case, that's the farmer. Even if you dig in your own back garden, you have to show the coroner. I think if it's over three hundred years old. And if it's treasure trove, then you definitely have to declare it. There are lots of rules.'

'I expect gold and bullion is buried around here,' said David, as he tied the puppy's leash to the handle of the wheelbarrow.

'Well–' began Rhys.

Tara smiled to herself as she heard David outlining his plans for discovering a hoard of gold and silver in the valley.

'Have you been to the standing stones and the well?' asked Isabelle, who was working next to her.

'Not yet. We cycled past the stones to get here, but this is our first day. By the way, Suzi and Ben Harris are our parents. They said you might be here. So – this is us – exploring!'

'Exploring lots of molehills!' laughed Isabelle. 'My brother and I–' she pointed across to Rhys– 'we live opposite you, across the river.'

The girls smiled at each other.

'Come canoeing with us sometime.'

'Cool.'

'Over there is a well. It's called St Anne's Well. If you go across the road, it's in the field on the other side of that red van. It's supposed to be a healing well; it's been used for hundreds of years, maybe thousands.'

'Wow!' said Tara, as she ran her fingers over the earth, feeling for anything underneath. *This is better than using a trowel*, she thought.

'The standing stones were thrown by a hairy giant from Anglesey. So the story goes. He must have had a great aim! Good enough for the Olympics!'

They both laughed.

Isabelle stood up and stretched. 'I'll go and show Alan these fragments. He likes dating pottery. I expect they are 21st century picnic mugs, but I could do with a break!'

Tara picked up her trowel again. She could see Tabitha walking around with her clipboard, looking intent. *I don't think I've seen her actually working in a trench*, she smiled. As she moved her fingers over the next layer of earth, they touched something hard. There was a clinking sound.

'That could be a coin,' said Tabitha, coming up behind her. 'What is it?'

Say nothing, Tara heard a whisper in her head.

She quickly picked up a pebble. 'It's only a stone,' she replied. 'If I find some pottery, I'll wash it in this bucket, shall I?'

'Yes. And be careful. Use a toothbrush.' Tabitha tapped on her clipboard. 'Remember, I need to log everything, every find. Throw the stones on that pile over there.'

Tabitha waddled off to another trench, carefully picking her way around the molehills.

Tara could hear Alan telling his group about the Marcher Lords of Wales. 'This area all around here belonged to Lord John of Gaunt. Monmouth was a favourite castle of his. Tintern Abbey owned vast acres of land here, and St Briavels Castle is across the river. Has anyone visited it?'

David was feeling hot, hungry, and very bored. Alan's voice droned on and on.

Looking over at his sister, he noticed she was bending over the trench and staring at something.

Then she glanced around to see if anyone was looking. David started to call, 'Ta–'

She shook her head and sent a mind-message. *Don't ask.*

Maybe she's found something interesting, thought her twin. *I hope so! Not that we can keep it.*

'There had been harsh laws against the Welsh since Edward l began his invasion of the country in 1277...'

'Excuse me. Is it time for lunch yet, Alan?' asked David, keen to see what his sister had discovered.

The rest of the group grinned as the archaeologist stopped and checked his watch.

'I suppose it is.'

'It's just that I probably need to take our puppy for a long walk, and I don't want to be late back.' David smiled, saint-like, at Alan. This usually worked with his teachers.

'Yes, alright, you can go. We'll carry on for another five minutes, and we can all break for an hour. Now, where was I? Oh, yes... The Marcher Lords were mainly away in Ireland in the late fourteenth century, fighting. They were absentee landlords, so their stewards looked after their lands...'

David untied the spaniel quickly from the wheelbarrow. He could see Tara hunched over, brushing earth off something. The puppy dashed towards the woods.

'Bethan! Come back!' he shouted, waving the leash.

Tara was staring down at a bag made of some soft material. Could it be fur or wool? On it was an image of an animal, slinky and slender. Very gently, she pressed the oval shape. There was something hard inside.

Then came a whisper:

Here is the Otter who lives between this world and the next.

Protecting you from all dangers,
On land and sea, in valleys and rivers,
Living between this world and the next,
Twisting and sliding with freedom and courage.

There was a silence.

The Bronze Mirror is for you to keep and use, for you only, to fulfil the quest.

Tara glanced around the field and noticed that everyone was busy in their trenches, or discussing coins and pieces of pottery they'd found that morning. She took out her bottle of water and, as she did so, slipped the bag into her backpack. She was taking some sips, wondering what she had found, when a shadow fell over her from behind.

'Have you got something interesting there?' asked Toby. He was staring at her backpack.

'My lunch! A bottle of water, and some sandwiches. Gosh, I'm famished,' laughed Tara. 'And hot too, aren't you?' She wiped her forehead with the back of her hand.

The boy looked suspiciously at her. 'We have to show everything we find. You know that, don't you? That's the rule. We must keep the rules.'

'Yep. Got that,' said Tara as she looked around for her brother and cousin. *We need to get away from here and see what's inside the bag. Away from prying eyes.*

'Have you found anything exciting today?'

'Er – no,' he muttered, as he sidled away towards a pile of roof tiles lying by a wall.

Simone was showing Tabitha a coin. 'Is it important? Or can I keep it?'

'We'll see at the end of the day. Put it on the table in the tent for now.'

The archaeologist sighed. It had felt like quite a long day already, with these new volunteers and their yappy dog. 'It must be time for lunch.'

Bethan ran back into the field, and was jumping and barking up at Toby. David arrived, out of breath after chasing her around the village.

'Take your dog, and walk it around for a good hour. Go to the church, over to the stones, or the well. All of them! Perhaps that will wear it out,' said Paul. 'It's a nuisance.'

Simone frowned. '*No!* She's a puppy. She's lovely.'

Tara tugged at her cousin's arm. 'Lunch! I'm hungry.'

'Me too,' said her cousin. She glared at the man as they walked away.

David clipped the leash onto the spaniel's collar. 'Walk to heel, Bethan.'

'Come on. Let's go to the well, and have our lunch there. We'll see what Dad's given us. It could be pizza,' said Tara.

'Cold pizza?' asked her cousin. '*No!*'

'*Andi - Andi!*' shouted David as the puppy dragged him off towards the gate.

'*Andiamo!*' called Simone. 'Let's go!'

'Can we ban that dog from this afternoon's dig?' Paul said in a loud voice.

'Chill! It's only for another few hours,' said Ruth. 'I don't think they are coming back tomorrow. It's no big deal.'

'I'll tell them they can't come back,' snapped Tabitha. 'They'll never find anything. Not like Toby.'

Bethan could be heard barking in the distance, as the children raced towards the well.

'You're going to have to train her, David,' said Tara, panting.

'Tomorrow. There's always tomorrow.'

☆☆☆ Chapter 3
At the Well

'Oh, look! Colours on the trees,' said Simone. Thin strips of ribbons tied to branches were waving in the breeze. '*Bellissimo!* Beautiful!'

David was reading the notice by the wooden gate. 'It says this is a healing well. People have been coming here for hundreds of years, to get some of the water. You can drink it, or put it on your wound, or the bit of you that hurts, and then you get better. The ribbons are for – OK – I'm not sure about whether you tie them on *when* you ask for help, or *afterwards,* when you are cured. Hang on.'

David continued reading, while Bethan sniffed around the steps leading down to the well.

'Right. Dip the material in the water. Tie it to a tree, and ask the saint, or spirit of the water, to help you.'

'Do you believe it?' asked Simone. 'My grandmother in Egypt has the eye to keep evil spirits away.'

'Nanny Lita has prayer beads,' said David.

Tara looked around, to make sure that no one else was there. She took out the bag, which still had some bits of earth clinging to it. She shrugged. 'If people believe something works, why not? It's ancient, isn't it? Anyway, it's good to respect other people's faiths. Who says what we believe is right? Question everything. Always.'

An image of the Goddess flashed into her mind. *Remember the quest.* She mind-messaged to her twin. They smiled at each other. *Ah, yes. Now we remember...*

Simone walked down the steps. 'I'll put some of this water on my eyes. They are very sore, after digging in that field for hours.' She dipped her wristband in the water.

David grimaced. It had been a year since they had seen their cousin, and so far, she had complained about everything. Was it going to be a very long summer?

Tara breathed long and deeply. 'Good idea. Bathe your eyes and eyelids in the water.'

'*Si.* Yes. I'll put my wristband on that branch. Mamma gave it to me, so it is very special.'

'You could drink the water, too. Then all of you would be cured.'

Tara gave her twin The Look and signalled "zip".

Simone was tying the blue and yellow threads around a twig. 'All – *non capito* – I don't understand.'

'He means if you drank the water, it would be

good for you,' said Tara quickly. She smiled at her cousin. 'Why don't we all ask for something special, tie a ribbon – or some material – on a twig, and drink the water?'

'Bethan, too!' said David, as he bent over the well and cupped his hands. 'She'd ask for plenty of food!'

'*Bene*. Good. I'll ask for a – an awesome summer.'

Her cousins grinned. 'Perfect!'

Simone finished tying her wristband, and examined the ribbons dangling from the low-hanging branches.

'Anyway, Twin. You've got something to tell us. I know that special look of yours.'

The spaniel was at the bottom of the mossy steps, lapping up the water. Simone bent down next to her and splashed some drops on her eyes. 'Do you think this water is clean? Pure?'

'Definitely,' replied David. 'Especially after Bethan has…' Then he saw Tara take something out of her backpack. 'What's that you've got? More sandwiches?'

'No! I found this bag in the trench. I was told to keep it. It's a great secret. So please do not tell anyone about this. Ever. It's important – I don't know why.'

'But we must give it to the arch– those people – it is the rule.'

David sighed. 'Just because they say it's the rule, it doesn't mean we have to follow it then and there – not immediately.'

Simone looked puzzled. 'We don't?'

'No, we don't,' said David. 'There may be – extraordinary circumstances. And if Tara says it's a secret. Then we keep *schtum*.'

'*Schtum?* What is *schtum?*' Simone smiled. 'Oh Yes! The same! Silent.'

'Exactly.'

'We say nothing,' said Tara. 'We must be careful what we say to people. Are we agreed? Have we a pact?' She put out her right hand, with her palm facing downwards.

David put his right hand on top of his sister's. 'Yes.'

Their cousin looked at them. They were serious. She tentatively put out her right hand, and placed it on top of theirs.

Tara placed her left hand over it. 'Now our pact is sealed. Our lips are sealed.' She picked up the bag, and brushed some soil from it.

'Look!' said her twin. 'There's a picture of an animal. It could be an otter.'

'Ott–?'

'It swims in rivers, and catches fish.' David waved his hand from side to side, in a slippery, twisting motion.

'Oh... *lontra*. They are special. Sacred...'

Tara opened the bag and brought out the object.

'Cool! That's metal. Is it bronze?'

'Yes, it's a mirror.'

Placing her hand just above the oval mirror, Tara

moved it clockwise three times, very slowly.

Came the whisper, **_The journey between the worlds begins..._**

'It seems to be an ancient mirror,' said Tara quietly.

'A bronze mirror,' murmured her brother.

'I love mirrors,' said Simone. 'Can I see? I think I need to tidy my hair. My plait's coming loose.'

She reached over to take it from her cousin.

'Let me look first.' David tried to snatch it.

Tara drew back from them both, and held the Bronze Mirror tightly to her heart.

'Neither of you can have it. No one can use it except me,' she said. 'Otherwise, it won't work. It has something to tell us. It's to help us. We have to do something. Go somewhere. The Goddess gave us a special task; a quest to fulfil.'

Simone was furious. 'I don't see why only you can have this Mirror.'

'That's how it is. We made a pact. And we have to trust each other. Always. Whatever happens. There's something important that needs to be done. We three have been chosen. So – there's to be no JAR: no JEALOUSY, no ANGER, no RESENTMENT. Otherwise, our quest will not be fulfilled.'

'This is cosmic!' said David. 'Just chill, Simone. You made a wish for an awesome summer. Here we are! How cool is this?'

Tara looked seriously at them both.

'We're a team. Each one of us has to play our part on this journey. Simone, you've been chosen for this quest, too. It means you are very important in all this.'

Her cousin looked pleased. 'So why has this... this Mirror... appeared?' What is this quest? What do we have to do? Where will we go?'

'I don't know exactly,' said Tara. 'Not yet. Let's look.'

They stared into the Bronze Mirror; swirls of blue and green, spiralling, reaching down, down, into depths unknown. A glimpse of the Goddess. She smiled, then vanished; once more, the Mirror reflected only drifting shapes.

Bethan rolled over, barked, and sat up. They all laughed.

'And now – lunch!' said David.

'Good. I'm starving.' As Tara placed the Mirror in the bag, she noticed a design had been carved into its back. Spirals.

'That's beautiful,' she murmured.

'We've only got an hour before we have to be back at the dig,' said Simone. She was feeling special now, even though she didn't understand what all this was about. An adventure. A journey. *I've already been on a journey*, she thought, little knowing what was about to happen.

'Egg and tomato sandwiches. My favourite,' said Tara, as she unpacked her lunchbox.

They lay on their backs, staring up at the clear

blue sky. White lines, traces of planes, were being drawn way above them.

Stones, stones, circle of stones, cyclch cerrig, the whisper came.

'We must go to the circle of standing stones now. We saw them when we cycled here,' said Tara, as they finished munching their apples. 'Come on. Yes, you too, Bethan.'

'Why?' asked Simone.

David and Tara ran on ahead. The spaniel bounded off in front of them. 'Because!' they shouted together. 'Just because! Race you!'

Arriving at the entrance, the twins jostled each other to see who could get through the metal gate to the field first.

'Do you think she's going to be alright?' asked David as he squeezed himself in front of Tara. 'I might get really fed up with her. She's being a bit of a pain, even you have to admit that.'

'A – she's our cousin. B – she's our guest, and she's here for a reason. C – we have to learn to get on with people in life, even if we don't like them. Mum and Dad are always saying that. And D – David! Everyone has annoying habits – even you!'

They dropped their backpacks by the hedge and punched each other playfully. Bethan jumped around them, wagging her tail.

'I haven't got one bad habit,' he laughed. 'But you've got lots, my big twin sister!'

Simone appeared.

'Don't fight,' she begged. 'Please don't fight. I hate people fighting. Mamma and Papa always are.'

David and Tara exchanged looks. They had overheard their parents saying their aunt and uncle were having problems. That's why Simone was with them for the whole summer.

'We're playing. We're just pretending,' said Tara. 'Everything's cool.'

'Cool, chilled. And I am so hot.' Simone turned away to read the notice board by the gate.

'Oh, here's the story. They're called Harold's Stones. A giant threw these when he was playing a game with the Devil. They were having a competition, and the stones landed in a circle.' She looked over at the three standing stones: two were upright, and one was leaning in a different direction. 'That is a very strange story. I don't believe it.'

The whisper came: ***Take the Bronze Mirror. Walk around the stones; follow the hands of a clock. Around, around, around.***

Tara took the Mirror out of the bag. 'The quest begins... Let's walk around the stones. Bethan, too.'

The spaniel pricked up her ears, her eyes starting to roll. She raced wildly around the field, barking and howling.

'Bethan!' shouted Tara.

'She must sense something.' David caught the puppy, and put her on a tight leash.

Tara held the Mirror in both hands as they walked around the stones in single-file. Slowly, deliberately, they circled the three standing stones: once, twice, three times. A light breeze touched their faces. In the far corner of the field, branches of the ancient oaks swayed. Clouds gathered and turned a dark blue-grey. In seconds, strong gusts of wind sent them racing across the sky.

A storm? wondered Tara.

Touch the tallest stone, came the whisper.

After they completed the circle, Tara put out her right hand and placed it on the leaning stone. Instantly, there was a flash, and she was flung back. She lay on the ground as a powerful wind whirled around her. Clutching the Mirror to her heart, she felt the earth beginning to shake. Was the ground about to split open? Were they going to be sucked down? Fall through a crack in the Earth's crust? Then, almost immediately, she was caught up, tossed and spun around like a feather.

'What's happening?' she shouted. 'David! Simone!'

The whisper came louder now.

Worlds are colliding.

Feel the vortex.

Do not be afraid.

Do not feed the Fear.

Tara felt as if she were spinning forever, in the

middle of a hurricane. 'When will this end? I can't breathe. There's nothing to hold on to – except the Bronze Mirror.'

'Tara! David! Help!' From a distance, Tara could hear Simone screaming. She tried to speak to her to calm her, but no words came.

The next moment, she was floating above the planet, sliding in and out of time. Faces came towards her: faces with fierce and angry eyes. Men with swords, charging across deserts. Mongol warriors! The wind dropped.

Tara fell to the ground by the first stone. She turned over and stared at the cloudless sky. Swallows darted overhead; two red butterflies were playing chase. The sound of bees buzzing from one buttercup to the next filled the meadow. A line of beeches stood where the hedge had been before the storm.

'I don't remember seeing beeches this afternoon,' she murmured. 'Oaks. There were oaks. Even the flowers look different. Or am I imaging things?'

David and Simone had been flung over near the trees. They lay on the ground. Bethan was trying to lick David's face.

'Ergh–' said Simone. 'That's–'

'Yukky. OK. But we are alive, and all in one piece.' He glanced around, to see where his twin was. 'What a storm! Still breathing?'

'In and out. Very slowly!'

'Was it an earthquake, or a tornado?' He sat up

and noticed there were lots more trees.

'Beeches. Where did they come from? And I've never seen these red, spiky flowers before.'

'It's tranquil here now,' said Simone. 'No planes. No cars.'

Tara sniffed the air. 'But I can smell wood burning.' She was puzzled. 'I don't remember there being a fire.'

On this still, midsummer afternoon, a woodpecker was busy hammering at a tree trunk, a cuckoo called, thrushes sang high up amongst the newly-greened leaves.

Stretching her arms out wide, Simone gazed up at the sky. 'Those long white lines – they've disappeared.'

'Everything feels different, looks different, smells different. Was that a hurricane? What do you think, Tara?'

David's twin sat on the grass, peering into the Bronze Mirror. As she looked into it, she saw her hair was still light red-brown and straight, but it was much shorter. She felt different. Glancing over at her twin, she noticed that his hair was dark, but not as curly. Odd. What had happened? Simone's hair was still dark, but she didn't have a plait now; it looked shorter, too. And Bethan? She was exactly the same.

Putting her head on one side, she pricked up her ears, and she began to howl.

'Bethan! Stop! That's a terrible noise!' said David

crossly as he stood up and brushed grass from his leggings. 'Why am I wearing this?' he asked. He was wearing a loose tunic.

Simone had jumped up, and was staring at their clothes. 'These are old things!' she wailed. 'Horrible! Big! I don't like these. Is this a joke? Leggings. I hate leggings.'

Then she touched her hair. 'It's short! Where's my long hair? Did you cut it?' She glared at David. 'I want to go home. This is terrible. I hate it here!'

Instead of the clothes they had put on that morning, the three of them were wearing rough brown woollen tunics and leggings, with leather shoes.

'OMG! Why...?' began David.

Simone started sobbing. '*Non capito.* I don't understand. *Mamma, mamma!*'

'Shush. Listen,' said Tara.

The sound of a girl singing was being carried on the breeze, across the meadow.

Tara mind-messaged her twin. *Now,* she said, *our quest begins.*

Chapter 4
Carys appears

'*Bore da.*' A young girl, with dark brown, wavy hair, tied back with a blue ribbon, was walking towards them. She was carrying a small pot.

'Er – *Bore da.* Good morning,' said Tara.

The girl stood and stared at them. 'You have come. You have come.' Her voice was soft and musical. '*Diolch.* Thank you,' she smiled. 'Come with me to the well first. Mother needs the water. You know she is sick. Then we must go to the castle and search for it. Everything will be all right now.'

While Bethan ran over to the stranger to be patted, Simone looked at her cousins. 'Who is this girl? Where are we? What's going on? How does she know us? What is "it"?' she asked.

Go with her, came the whisper from the Mirror.

'Let's go then,' said Tara.

The twins started to follow, but Simone froze. She stared at the girl, who was already turning to go down a track; one that she hadn't noticed before.

'Name. What's your name?' she managed to ask.

'Carys. And you're Simone. You live in a place with seven hills, and fallen-down buildings. Strange shapes.'

The girl from Rome couldn't utter a word. Then Carys pointed to David and Tara.

'You're Tara. And your name's David.'

He nodded. 'What's going on—? Why?'

'Questions! In my dream, you were always asking questions!' said Carys, and laughed.

'What about?' he smiled as she patted the puppy.

There was a flash of light from Tara's hand. 'You have brought the Mirror,' said Carys. 'That is good. Last night, it was the new moon. A time of beginnings. I was sitting with Mother. She was hot, so hot. She has been sick for a week now. Then I fell asleep and dreamt. In my dream, three friends came: two girls, a boy, and a small dog. You, Tara, you told me that you were coming to help us. You had been sent. And here you are. You will help us. I know you will. First, though, we must go to St Anne's Well.'

Carys strode on ahead down the track.

Tara took hold of Simone's arm and said, 'We have to go with her. Come on. I don't know why we are here. But we'll find out.'

'Maybe it has to do with the Mirror,' said David. 'The quest—'

'The quest — for what? I don't understand…'

'Neither do I, but we made a pact. And that is that. The Bronze Mirror was found for a reason.

We'll go with Carys now, and find out why we are here – wherever "here" is – and what's going on.' Tara turned and called back to her twin. 'How's your first aid?'

'A bit patchy, actually. If someone's heart has stopped beating, I know how to do CPR to *Staying Alive*.'

'Why? What?' Simone looked confused. 'Are we here to save her mother's life?'

'I'm not sure, but let's see,' said Tara, as she put the Mirror inside the soft fur bag. She was hoping it would whisper the answer, but there was no sound. Only silence.

They arrived at St Anne's Well. Now it was surrounded by patches of earth. Tall grasses, thistles, and cow-parsley swayed in the warm summer breeze.

Carys put down the small pot, took the piece of blue ribbon from her hair, dipped it in the water, and tied it to a hanging branch. Kneeling at the top of the stone steps, she closed her eyes and put her hands together.

'Please heal my mother,' she pleaded. 'Her name is Eva ap Morgan, and there are three children. Owen, our father, died, and James, our eldest brother, too. Our family are potters, and have been for many years, making the tiles for the castles and the abbeys. But now the great lord, John of Gaunt, who owns these lands, has taken them from us. We do not understand why. What can we do? Where will we go? We have to leave our land in seven days. We will be without a home. Heal our mother, please. Give us back our land. I beg you to help us. I am here praying for a miracle.'

Tara, David and Simone listened in horror. This wasn't just about a sick woman with a temperature. This was a lot more complicated. How could they solve all these problems? Carys believed that they could and they would. She believed they had been sent to do exactly that. But who was this Lord John?

Simone noticed something. Her wristband – the one that she had tied to a branch near the well about half an hour ago – wasn't there. Neither were the other coloured ribbons that she'd seen on the other trees. She turned to her cousins: 'My wristband isn't there. Where has it gone?'

'I wish you'd worry about other things, and not just yourself,' blurted out David.

'We – you–'

'Shush,' said Tara. 'She means *why* isn't it there? What is going on? Those thick brambles by the entrance weren't here ten minutes ago. Think, David. Carys said "John of Gaunt". Who's he? Does he own the land around here?'

'I don't know. Maybe he's a local farmer. Alan the archey was going on about him. I wasn't really listening. All I know is we are living in Wales now, on the Borderlands: the Welsh Marches. That's what Mum said. We can walk from Wales to

England from our front gate. We saw the sign. It only takes a minute. Hop over the border. Here one minute and gone the next!'

Simone glared at her cousin. 'What are you talking about – we are gone? Gone? Where are we? Will anyone come to look for us? Who is this farmer John?' Her eyes filled with tears.

'We'll find out, bit by bit,' Tara hugged her cousin. 'Just think. You can write a story for your school magazine.'

'There is no magazine!' Simone hissed. 'I made it up, so I didn't have to dig holes for that – that ridiculous woman!'

Carys came back with her pot full of water from the well. 'I'll bathe my mother's head with this, and then she'll be cured.'

'Cross fingers,' murmured David. His sister pressed her finger firmly into his back. 'Ouch!'

Bethan was scampering along the path, snuffling in the undergrowth, pushing over stones and small branches.

'Let's go to my home now. We can stay there tonight, and take the tiles to the steward at the castle tomorrow morning. We'll have to leave at sunrise.'

'What tiles? Which castle?' choked Simone. She felt lost. Where was she? Why did Tara seem calm, and David keep making jokes? And who exactly was this girl? 'Which castle?' she almost screamed.

Carys turned to Tara. 'You haven't told them?'

'I don't know everything,' she answered. 'The Mirror only whispers little bits to me.'

They were following Carys along the narrow path, and past the standing stones.

There are no hedges, thought David. *Meadows full of buttercups and blue and pink flowers, butterflies with speckles or pale yellow. Lots of oaks and ash trees, beeches and birches.* He mind-messaged his twin. *How stunning is this?*

'Home is along here, and partway down the hill. Did you come up that way?' asked Carys.

'Yes, we pushed our cycles up, and rode them along to the field,' said David.

'Cycles? What are they?'

'Well, they have two wheels–'

She turned around, trying not to spill the water. 'Like carts?'

'Kind of–' Tara said quickly.

'Well–' David began, then caught his sister's glance. 'Er – yes.'

The smell of burning wood had become stronger as they trudged on down a slope. On either side, the trees grew densely, until suddenly a clearing opened up. In the middle stood a small thatched cottage, with a fence around it. There were some water butts and piles of firewood; a few wooden sheds were nearby.

Two small children were running around, chasing each other with twigs. A young boy of about ten years old was sitting on a tree stump, playing a tune on a whistle.

'Hugh! How is Mother?'

'She's sleeping now. I played her some of my songs.' He got up awkwardly, and stared at the three visitors and their dog.

'*Ciao,*' said Simone.

The boy looked confused. '*Bore da.*'

'This is Tara, David and Simone,' said Carys, pointing to each one. 'And that's Bethan.'

The spaniel bounded up to the boy and sat looking up at him with her large, soulful eyes. Stroking her head, he stared at each visitor in turn.

'I told you they would come, Hugh. They'll prove this land is ours.' She smiled. 'They can speak to Lord John and Lady Katherine. Then they will understand that we are free people.' She turned to Tara. 'First, let me put this water on Mother's head and face.'

David was staring at Hugh. He seemed familiar. Had he met him before? His hair was light red, and his eyes were blue.

'Are you a page?' the young boy asked.

'No.' David mind-messaged his twin. *Does he think I'm part of a book?*

Tara shook her head at her brother.

'So – you can help us?' Hugh walked across to them. 'Are you the son of a lord? Does your father know John of Gaunt? Or the king? If you don't, how can we get our land back?'

The young boy was now looking quite angry.

John of Gaunt? That name again. *Who **is** he?* wondered Tara.

He's the uncle of the king, came the whisper from the Mirror.

But which king? She mind-messaged her twin. *There must have been a time shift? Are we on a different planet? Have we found a portal into another galaxy?*

Perhaps we've stumbled onto a film set, David messaged back. *Are we in England or Wales? Or some other country?*

It's all getting too confusing, she answered. *My head is starting to spin. You ask him.*

'Who is the king?' asked David.

Hugh frowned. 'You don't know? Everyone knows that.' He looked scornfully at him. 'The King of England is Richard. Richard the Second.' He glanced furtively around, and lowered his voice. 'They say he hates his uncle, John of Gaunt. And John of Gaunt's son, Henry Bolingbroke, even more. Perhaps there will be war.' His eyes gleamed. 'And here in Wales, our own prince, Owain Glyndwr, is gathering men even now, to fight against the king. We have a great leader.' He stared at them. 'Have you been sent here by our prince?'

Carys came out from the cottage. 'Hugh! Shush! You know Father always told us we must never repeat stories about Lord John, or King Richard. It is treason; we could be hung. And say nothing about our prince.' She put her finger to her lips. 'Nothing!'

Simone looked terrified. 'Hung? Killed? Where are we? What year is this?'

'You have come to the Welsh Marches, and it's the seventeenth year of the reign of Richard II,' answered the girl. '1398.' She took her brother's arm and led him away towards the sheds, speaking so quietly they couldn't hear.

'Monumental!' said David. 'Richard II. Who is he? Or rather – who *was* he? I've never heard of him. Do you think we are stuck here forever, in some black wormhole?'

'*O Dio mio!*' wailed Simone. 'How will we ever get back to our time? What will our parents do?'

Tara put her arm around her cousin. 'Try not to look shocked. They're counting on us to help them. We've been sent here to get their land back. We can do it. Let's be brave and go with it. The Bronze Mirror–'

'It's the Mirror that has got us into this,' said Simone, kicking at a tuft of grass.

'And it will get us out,' said Tara firmly. 'It's an adventure. Jump in!'

'*O Dio*–'

'Come and eat,' said Carys. '*Croeso.* Welcome.'

'Great. I'm starving,' said David, as he tied Bethan's leash around a tree.

'Sit. Good girl. Stay.'

The trio went inside the cottage. It was small and dark, though the embers of a fire still glowed. In the corner, on a rush mattress, a woman was sleeping. The small pot of water was next to her. Her children were taking it in turns to bathe her forehead.

'This is our mother, Eva ap Morgan, and Meghan and Liam.'

Tara smiled at the children as the trio went over and sat by the fire.

'Here's some bread and cheese for you.' Hugh handed a platter to Simone.

'And some ale,' said Liam.

Simone closed her eyes, murmuring, 'I wish this nightmare would just end.'

'Thank you very much,' said Tara. 'In our part of the country, we are not used to ale. Could we have some water, please?'

'I'd like–' started David but stopped as he caught his twin's Look.

'And we have potage,' said Hugh pointing to a bowl on the fire. 'Cabbages, onions and leeks. Yesterday, I put a rabbit in it, and some parsley, too.'

Simone peered at it. 'It's green,' she muttered. 'I'll be sick.'

'Bread and cheese. That's very good, thank you,' said Tara quickly.

Simone was poking at the brown bread. She turned it over, looking for any mould.

'Ugh! I can't eat this. I might get food poisoning.'

'Manners,' said her cousin, nibbling at the dry edges.

'You won't. Anyway, if you do get worms, when we get back, just take some tablets! They'll probably come out in long strings,' David said, eating a lump of cheese. 'This tastes really good!'

'Worms? What are worms?' Simone asked as she turned the cheese around.

'Wiggerly wrigglers…' said David. 'Moving around your insides, your intestines…'

'Stop it, you two,' hissed Tara. 'We don't know how long we're going to be in this time, so just eat! We're going to need our strength, so don't be a wimp. Imagine it is the best pizza ever, and swallow it!'

As they sat around the fire, Simone continued to complain how smoky it was, how itchy her eyes were, and about the staleness of the bread.

Tara nudged her cousin. 'Shush, you are not helping here. Be more positive.' Turning to Carys, she asked, 'At the well, you said your father was a potter?'

The young Welsh girl threw some more kindling on the fire, and gazed into the flames as they spurted up. 'Our family have been potters for many years. Grandfather made the tiles for castles, abbeys, convents, and cathedrals, too. A master craftsman he was, travelling all around the Marches. Our father and James, our eldest brother, were potters too, but then they died so suddenly. Hugh and I were beginning to learn the skills from them.' She sighed. 'You saw our kiln on the way up the hill. Our tiles are beautiful, and the nobles for miles around desire them for their palaces; abbots for their churches and chapels.'

'What did they die of?' asked David.

Tara frowned at him. *It could be important*, he mind-messaged.

'They drowned. The river took them one night.'

'That's terrible.'

'Yes. it was.' Hugh scowled. 'The law is, if a tenant dies without making a will, all the property goes to the Lords of the Marches. Here, it goes to Lord John of Gaunt.'

'That's not fair!' said David as he took some more cheese.

'But Father did make a will. He left everything to Mother, to us,' said Carys.

'So this land is yours,' said Simone. 'Go to a lawyer, and it'll be fine.' She smiled around at everyone. 'That's that!'

Hugh broke in, 'But William Sargeant, the steward, has hidden the will. It's somewhere in Monmouth Castle. We don't know where. So, if we can't find it, we lose everything. We'll be homeless by the Feast day of St Peter and Paul.'

'Feast day?' said David.

'Today is midsummer, so it's in seven days' time,' explained Carys.

'Why would he do that?' asked Tara.

'So he can be in favour with the Lord.'

'And there's more,' said Hugh. 'He's building a manor house three miles from here, and everyone knows that he needs a lot of money.'

'It's unjust!' said David, poking the fire with a piece of twig. 'We'll definitely help you find the will.'

'What must we do?' asked Simone. She stared around the cottage. It looked very bare.

'I'll explain later,' said Tara hurriedly.

'A day after Father's death,' Carys continued, 'William Sargeant came here with his clerk, Thomas ap Pryce, and several men. He told Mother that all our possessions had to be taken there and then, to Monmouth Castle. It is the law, he said. He told us we must leave our home, our kiln, our land, by St Peter and St Paul's Day.' Carys choked back tears. 'Mother begged him. "We are potters. We need our kiln, we make tiles and live here quietly. We are free. We are not peasants, not serfs. This is our land."'

'Then,' said Hugh, 'Thomas ap Pryce spoke up, saying it wasn't our land any longer, that it belongs to Lord John of Gaunt. And he, a fellow Welshman, treating us like slaves.'

'Shush,' Carys touched her brother's arm, and looked over to their mother. 'Thomas the clerk told the men to take everything. He produced a document with the Lord's seals.'

'William Sargeant said there were tiles that Father owed him. They have to be taken to the castle this week.' Hugh sighed. 'We must deliver them before we leave here – forever.'

'They are for Queen Philippa's chamber,' said Carys. 'As Lord John and Lady Katherine are coming this month, the tiles must be laid, and all made ready for them. We have no choice.'

'Queen Philippa? Who's she?' asked Simone, suddenly interested. 'Can we meet her?'

David rolled his eyes. 'I expect she'll invite us to tea!'

'She was the mother of Lord John.' Carys paused. 'We could ask to see Lady Katherine. I have heard her heart is full of kindness. They will be returning to the castle, but it might be too late for us.'

Eva turned over on her rush mattress and groaned. Liam bathed her head with the water from the well, while Meghan stroked her hand.

Carys looked over at them. 'That was some days ago, and then Mother became ill. So we are just surviving here. It's very difficult.'

'We must take these tiles to the castle tomorrow,' said Hugh. 'We have no choice. '

'Will you come with us? Then we can all search for the will.'

'Yes, of course,' said Tara. She stared at her cousin. 'We'll help, won't we, cuz?'

'How far is it?' asked Simone. 'Is it a very long way?'

'Only four or five miles. Along to Penallt, and down the hill to Monmouth,' said Hugh.

The girl from Rome sighed, and continued gazing into the fire.

'What happens if we are discovered?' asked David.

'They will put us in the dungeons,' said Carys. 'It is dangerous.'

'*O Dio mio!*' Simone threw up her hands. '*No!* No! This is not for us – Tara –'

Hugh's face turned a fiery red. 'They should not steal our home from us. They should not take our land from us. Those nobles – they have so much. But we, we who are free but poor, have so little. It's not fair.'

'*Vita...* Life – it is not fair–' began Simone, and stopped as Tara gave her The Look.

'We're in, Hugh. Justice must be done,' said David firmly. 'We'll help you in any way we can.'

That night, as she tried to sleep, Tara turned over everything that had happened in the last few hours: getting to the dig; discovering the Bronze Mirror; the well; the standing stones; the storm; meeting Carys, then Hugh and the family. Was this real? Was this a dream? She looked over at Eva tossing and turning on her mattress, and the family sleeping nearby. She knew this wasn't a dream. This was real. They were here in the Welsh Marches. It was the seventeenth year of the reign of Richard II, and she couldn't remember anything about him. Was he a good king? Or a tyrant? She held the bag to her heart, caressing the image of the otter and murmuring, 'Guide us. Help us. Protect us.'

☆☆☆ Chapter 5

To Monmouth

Tara woke as Hugh crept quietly out of the cottage. A few shafts of light came through the open door. She could see Simone lying completely still on her back, with her eyes shut, her body taut, her breathing shallow.

She knew that her cousin was still in shock.

'Breathe deeply, Simone,' Tara whispered sleepily.

David came in and sat next to his twin. 'Hugh showed me the privy. It's by the trees and a bit smelly, but there's nowhere else.'

'I'll wait till we get to the castle,' said Simone, sitting up. 'They must have loos.'

'Maybe they won't have any there, either. Just squat in the bushes,' said David impatiently.

'I want to go home,' muttered his cousin. 'I hate it here.'

There was a low moan. Carys was bathing her mother's head. 'I think she's a bit better,' she whispered. 'I'll ask Rhiannon, our neighbour, to stay with her while we take the tiles to the castle. Can we guide the cart down the hill to the town together? The path is very bumpy.'

Hugh came back inside. 'All the tiles for the Queen's chamber are loaded,' he said. 'I did them all by myself, just now.'

'We'd have helped you,' smiled David. *A page?* he'd mind-messaged his sister the previous evening. *No! I'll be a squire. Or a knight! Arise, Sir David! What are the rules?*

Tara had laughed. *Be chivalrous. Especially to girls and women.*

Really?

Really. And be kind. Always.

That can't be it. They all go around killing everyone...

I don't think we've been brought here to murder people.

You never know. He'd turned over on the rush mattress, and had gone to sleep.

After washing their hands and faces, they ate some bread with honey, then the twins and Simone walked over to the cart.

'The path down to Monmouth may be muddy, as we had storms a few nights ago. Be careful not to slip,' said Carys.

Simone was picking up the tiles. 'These are very beautiful. Here's a fish, and a snake–'

'That one's an otter,' said Hugh.

'–and a deer. This looks like a big bird.'

'That's an eagle,' said Hugh. He was beginning to realise these visitors didn't know very much about a lot of things. *I can teach them*, he thought, and instantly felt better about himself.

People made fun of the young boy, because he was thin and small. He couldn't run as fast, or work for as long, as the other children. Learning to be a potter he enjoyed, and making up songs, too.

'We'll take some bread and cheese with us. And, before we go, here's some more water. It's going to be a hot day.' Carys passed Simone the one mug they had.

The young girl noticed some bits floating in it, pretended to take a sip, and handed it quickly to David.

'If you get dizzy from not drinking enough water, don't moan to me, cuz,' he muttered.

Time to be the peacemaker – again, thought Tara. *So tiring!* Aloud, she said, 'Oh, you've got lambs. Are they late arriving this year? Isn't spring the right time?'

'Lambs? No, they're our sheep!' said Hugh.

'They look a lot smaller than ours,' said David. 'But–' he saw the boy glaring at him and added, 'they look great, just great. And I love the pigs.'

Hugh grinned. 'So do I.'

Treading on eggshells here, David mind-messaged his sister. *Why is he so cross?*

I don't know, answered Tara. *Anyway, it's good for you! Practise being a patient page!*

Knight!

Meghan and Liam were collecting some firewood nearby as Rhiannon came into the clearing. Bethan raced towards her, and jumped up.

'*Bore da!* Good morning! Here are caps for you girls,' she said, as she fussed the puppy.

'Caps?' Simone was puzzled.

The woman held out three white pieces of cloth. 'I call them Monmouth caps. Put them on your head, and you'll all look like boys. You can't be going around the castle looking like girls. All the servants are boys. That'll be asking for trouble, and you don't want to invite it, *cariad*.'

Simone tucked her dark hair under the white cap. 'This could be quite the fashion. Maybe dyed different colours, and decorated with flowers.'

David raised his eyes to the sky, while Tara smiled her thanks at the neighbour.

'*Diolch*. Thank you, Rhiannon.'

'I'll mind Eva and the children. Come back safely.'

'I think the healing water is helping her,' said Carys.

'So,' said David. 'The plan is – deliver the tiles, search for the will, find it, and return here. Easy peasy!'

Hugh and Carys exchanged looks. 'Yes–'

'What? Is there something you haven't told us? Like a massive monster guarding the castle? Spells on the drawbridge? A curse?' David laughed.

'Well–' Carys looked as if she was going to say something, then stopped. 'I'll tell you later.' She disappeared into the cottage.

Tara held the bag with the Mirror tightly to her.

There is a secret, came the whisper. *A puzzle. Solve it with no anger, no jealousy, no fear.*

Simone was examining the tiles. '*Magnifico!* I'd like to learn how to make these.'

'I could teach you,' Carys said as she returned, and then exchanged glances with her brother.

'I'd like that.' Simone ran her fingertips over a swan. 'There are lots of birds. What are they all called?'

Hugh picked up some to show her. 'Here's an owl... a heron... a kingfisher...'

'Father used to make patterns mostly,' said Carys. 'I wondered why he made so many birds and animals of late.'

As everyone was getting ready to move off, Tara went into the woods and took the Mirror out of the bag. 'There's something that our friends aren't telling us. We know about the will, but they have a secret, too. Please show what's ahead,' she whispered. 'Warn us of any dangers.'

A swirl of grey mist passed over the glass.

Images came and went: thick stone walls; an angry man with cruel lips; long, embroidered curtains; an otter slipping into a fast-flowing river. And then — darkness.

What can this all mean? Tara wondered. *Shall we find the will? When can we go back to our time? Will we be missed?*

'Come on, Tara,' called her twin. 'We're off!'

Hugh sat on the cart, playing tunes on his bone whistle while the horse picked its way along the winding path. The woods on either side were thick and dense.

Bethan dived in and out of the trees, chasing whatever she could hear, smell, or thought she could see.

'What's she looking for?' David asked Hugh.

The boy paused between tunes. 'Boar — or pheasant. The men from the castle will have been hunting for rabbits, hares and other game, with Lord John returning. Lady Katherine comes hawking around here sometimes. In the old days, King John hunted in the Forest. His castle is over the river at St Briavels.'

He started another melody and Carys began to sing, '*Llef a roseson...*'

Simone hummed along to it.

We've fallen into an abyss, a black hole, haven't we? A parallel universe. David mind-messaged his twin.

We seem to have arrived in another time, she agreed. *There must be a portal, an entrance between our worlds, by Harold's Stones. Maybe this is happening while we are still on the dig at Trellech. Perhaps we are there, but we're here, too.*

David sighed. *Oh, that's too complicated. Do you think we'll get back to our time? We can't even phone 999!'*

Things will work out. You'll see. Tara smiled at him. *Here we are, in this beautiful place, on Midsummer's Day. Let's just go with it.*

David began humming the melody too. 'That's a brilliant tune, Hugh. Did you make it up?'

'Yes, I did.'

'So you are a potter?' Tara said. She wanted to find out more about the family. Perhaps she could discover their secret.

'Yes, I like making things: bowls, and tiles. And singing my songs, playing my whistle. And I'm learning the harp. Oh, the sound – lovely, it is. Then my mind goes away somewhere, and I can forget.'

David looked puzzled. 'Forget?'

'When I'm mocked for being so small,' he said. 'People can be so cruel.'

'But you have this amazing gift for music,' said

Tara. 'Ignore them. They're jealous. That's their problem, not yours.'

'I've never thought about it like that,' grinned Hugh, and he started another tune: jaunty and merry.

'He's our young bard,' smiled his sister. She tried to follow the melody as they all strolled along the muddy track.

'The storm brought down lots of branches the other night. Can you throw the bigger ones into the woods?' asked Hugh, as he guided the horse and cart down the hill. 'I don't want us to get stuck.'

'Sure.' David ran in front of the cart and threw a large stick into the ferns. The puppy stopped snuffling in the undergrowth and hurtled after it.

'No, Bethan! You'll only get it stuck in your mouth, and we'll have to take you to the vet — again.' He sighed. There would be no vet. Not yet.

The sun climbed higher and higher, drying out the earth, and leaving patches of damp mud. The wheels began to get stuck in the ruts.

Suddenly, the horse stopped. Hugh pulled at the reins, and the cart began to tilt sideways.

'Careful!' called his sister. 'Mind the tiles! None must get broken.'

'Push the cart forward then,' shouted the boy. 'Get it out of the rut! Quickly!'

Carys and the twins put their hands on the wooden slats on the back, and heaved. The wheels shot out and lurched to one side. The cart righted itself. The horse whinnied, shook his head, and plodded slowly on.

Tara glanced around. Where was Simone?

'Just needed a drink from the stream,' she said as she came out of the woods.

Our cousin isn't very keen on getting her hands dirty, Tara thought. *But she must be here for a reason.*

Not sure what it is exactly, her twin mind-messaged her.

They grinned at each other.

'What about you, Carys? What do you want to do?' asked Simone.

'Do?'

'With your life?'

'I make tiles – and pots, too. There's plenty of work here in the Marches.'

'But do you love it with a passion?' asked Simone.

Carys paused. 'A passion? I've never thought of it like that. I can do it, and I want to become a better potter. It is good, honest work. We can eat and survive. But – a passion? I'm not sure.'

'What else could you do?' Simone batted away a creeper that was dangling in front of them. 'If you decided to do something different, I mean.'

'I could join the nuns in the convent in Usk: pray, sew embroidered vestments and clothes for abbots, bishops and nobles, perhaps the king. Draw and colour illustrations on parchments...'

'Oh,' Simone frowned. 'Do you want to do that?'

'I'll be fourteen next year, and most girls get married then. I have choices.'

They don't sound like great choices to me, thought her new friend.

'When Mother is healed, and we have our land back, we'll go on a pilgrimage – to give thanks.'

'Come to Rome!' said Simone 'Come to Italy, and stay with me. It's so easy to get there – I'll take you to St Peter's Square, the Trevi Fountain–'

Tara shook her head and wondered whether her cousin had understood that they were now in 1398; that Richard II's time was completely different from their lives in the twenty-first century, and that they could soon be in great danger.

Carys smiled. '*Diolch*. Thank you, Simone. You are very kind.' She paused. 'But at the moment it is safer to travel in our own country here, in Wales. We'll go to St David's, and give thanks there.'

'Safer? Why?'

All around was peace: a blackbird was singing; two red squirrels were leaping from tree to tree; a dipper, perched on a mossy rock, sipped from the stream trickling alongside them.

Carys lowered her voice. 'There are rumours that our own prince, Owain Glyndwr, is preparing to fight, to take our country back from the English king, Richard II. Here, living in the Marches, we have to be watchful. Spies could be in these woods now. One careless word would bring trouble on us all.'

Simone stopped and listened intently. She was trying to grasp that she was living in the fourteenth century. 'Oh – I'm feeling a bit dizzy.'

'Drink some more water,' said Tara. 'It's getting hotter.'

'But – is it...?'

'Clean? Yes,' said her cousin, sighing heavily.

Hugh wiped the whistle on his sleeve. 'Where do you three come from?'

'Across the river,' David blurted out. 'Our parents have just bought a guest house. We're trying to think of a new name–'

He stopped abruptly, feeling that Tara was frowning at him.

He was right. 'Oh, look! Swallows!' he said hastily.

Across the clear blue sky, countless swallows were swooping, diving, turning in mid-air, catching, then gorging on, insects.

At least they're getting a good meal, he thought.

'I think Hugh is good enough to play at the feasts in the castle now,' said Carys, smiling at her brother. 'Father lets – er, *let*, him – play his tunes on market days.'

'Cool,' said David. 'Can you teach me to sing?'

'Oh no! You sound like a – a raven with a bad cold!' laughed his twin.

While Hugh taught his friend a new song, Carys talked about what they might see at the market that day in Monmouth. 'There may be minstrels, jugglers, acrobats; traders from France and Italy, as well. Their leather wares are beautiful.'

'That sounds exciting!' said Simone, as she patted her face with water. 'How much longer before we get there?'

An hour later, the children reached a clearing in the woods. Hugh pulled on the reins; the cart stopped. They stood on the brow of the hill overlooking Monmouth. From there, they could see two rivers: the Monnow, with the bridge and the gatehouse over it, and the Wye, flowing towards the sea. Swans, like specks of white, glided near the riverbank. Small boats swivelled and circled on the sparkling waters.

Looking across to the castle in the distance, they could see its strong, thick walls.

'Walls built to keep us out,' muttered Hugh.

The twins exchanged glances. Would they find the will? Would they get out of the castle without getting caught? Or would they be thrown into the dungeons, with no hope of escape?

☆☆
☆ Chapter 6
In the Castle

'Before we arrive at the castle, let's make a plan to get the will and your possessions back,' said Tara. 'We need to find out exactly where everything is hidden.'

'I heard tell that the goods of the dead, those who died of the plague, are stored in the cellar beneath the Great Hall,' said Hugh. 'But I'm not sure if that's true.'

'*O Dio mio!* So you *think* this document is in the cellar, or it could be somewhere else?' said Simone. 'And how can we get your things out without anyone seeing us?' She frowned at Carys and Hugh. 'If we did it in the middle of the night, someone will hear us carrying the things to the cart. If we did it during the day, everyone would see us.' She shrugged. 'Not possible. It is un – er, *im*possible. That's the truth, isn't it?'

The brother and sister exchanged worried glances.

'It won't be easy,' agreed the young Welsh girl.

'Come and sit in the shade, Simone.' Tara took her arm and guided her to the bank of the stream. 'The sun is beating down. Put some water on your head. Drink some...'

Her cousin glared. 'Don't talk to me like that. *There, there, poor Simone.*' She took off her cap and fanned herself. 'I'm fine. Just fine. Leave me alone!'

Tara stood back. Simone had eaten hardly anything, and she probably hadn't drunk enough water. *What should I do?* she wondered. *I feel it is my responsibility. Water. I'll get her some water...* She was looking around for a bowl when Carys spoke.

'The will is the most important thing to get.'

'We can do without all the other things,' sighed Hugh, as he thought of his harp, and how he loved to play it.

Carys sat down by Simone, and offered her some bread and cheese. 'You need to eat something, my friend.'

'*Grazie.* Thank you.'

Hugh had filled a bowl from the stream. 'Drink this.'

'Thank you. Both of you,' she whispered, as she sipped the cool water.

David mind-messaged his twin. *We definitely need a plan.*

Tara took a deep breath. 'Someone will have to stay outside the castle and look after the horse and cart – and Bethan.'

'Er–'

'No, she can't come in, Twin. After we've unloaded the tiles, she can guard the cart. Is there a place near the castle where she could stay?'

Bethan looked at each of them. What were they deciding to do with her? She began to whine.

Hugh patted the puppy. 'Don't worry. You and me. We'll stay by the Priory, and I'll look after you. Or the other way around.'

'Cool,' said David.

The spaniel jumped up, nuzzled Hugh's hand, and put her head on his lap.

'Friends!'

'Good. That's sorted,' said Tara.

'Reporting to William the steward,' said Carys. 'That's the first thing we must do.'

'William Sargeant?' David asked. 'The man who stole all your things?'

'Yes. We must deliver the tiles to him, and take them up to Queen Philippa's chamber,' said Carys. 'Then lay them.'

'Lay them?' muttered Simone. She examined her fingernails.

'If he knows we are searching the castle for the will, he'll do everything in his power to stop us,' said Carys. 'He and Thomas the clerk.'

'You'll have to search the whole castle,' said Hugh.

'How big is it?' asked David.

'Father said it has lots of rooms: the Great Hall, a chapel, a library...'

'The Great Tower.'

'We'll have to distract them, search all the rooms and find the document,' said David. 'Then run for it.'

Tara smiled at her brother. He thought it was going to be easy. She knew it wouldn't be. Glancing over at Carys, she noticed her new friend talking quietly to her brother. What were they keeping from them? Was it the secret the Mirror had whispered to her? Tara wasn't sure, but she knew there was something. They caught her eye, and quickly looked away. Guilt? Was that it? *What could they be feeling guilty about? That we are putting our lives in danger for them?* She could not read their minds.

David was thinking aloud. 'Maybe all the documents are fake, and it's a scam.'

'What's a scam?' said Hugh.

'Perhaps William and Thomas have forged lots of documents, and are going around telling people they must leave their homes. Then they take their land and possessions.'

'They'd need someone to write them and use Lord John's seal,' said Carys.

'They could be forged. The seal could be forged too,' said David, thinking of films he'd seen. 'Then when we find the documents, we can expose those two as thieves!'

Carys was trying to follow his thoughts. 'Or they could take the seal for some time and use it. Fix it to the bottom of a parchment.'

David frowned. 'Right.'

Tara sighed. 'Twin, your mind is running faster than a deer. Let's press pause, and breathe.'

'Ergh!' Her brother sat on the grass, closed his eyes, and started counting. 'In, two, three. Hold. Out, three, four, five.'

Carys started laughing. 'What are you doing?'

'Breathing deeply. It calms him down,' smiled Tara. 'His mind and emotions whirl around and around, like a tornado. This helps him. He sits and doesn't think – or speak – for a few minutes. It's restful – for everyone!'

'Like praying?'

'Er – kind of.'

'I'll try that,' said Simone, squeezing her eyes together.

'Let's all do it.'

'Great idea. We can lie down here in the shade and take five minutes to rest and breathe,' said Tara, touching her bag. 'Mirror, help us, please.'

Came the whisper:

Over the bridge to the place with stone walls

To seek in a chamber, in a tower, in the Great Hall...

Time stopped on this warm midsummer morning in 1398. There was little movement in the trees, just the softest of breezes. Murmuring sounds filled the air; water gushing, tumbling, a thrush's song.

Peace.

Tara was the first to sit up. The others, one by one, opened their eyes, as if they had been in a deep sleep.

'I have a plan,' said Tara. 'We arrive in Monmouth, make our way up to the castle, and ask for the steward. Hugh can say we've brought the tiles. Then we'll unload them, carry them up to—?'

'Queen Philippa's chamber. And lay them,' said Carys. 'There's a pattern we must follow.'

Simone rolled her eyes. This sounded like hard work!

'Afterwards, we'll split up and search the castle.'

'I'll look in the chapel,' said Carys.

'Simone and I will go to the Great Tower.'

'And I'll look in the kitchens.'

'No! The will won't be in the kitchens, Twin! Try the library.'

David sighed and turned to Hugh. 'Where's a good place to meet you and Bethan afterwards?'

'The Priory.'

'Right.'

'I want to come.' Hugh stroked the puppy's ears. 'But it's better if Bethan and I stay away from the castle. I'll leave the cart with Robert, the innkeeper. He lets me put it in his barn on market days so I can go off and see what's happening.'

'Does he then?' smiled Carys. Her brother looked sheepish.

David patted the spaniel. 'As long as she's got water and something to chew; a bone, maybe, she'll be happy. And don't bark, Bethan. Keep quiet.'

The puppy sat perfectly still, and looked saintly. *They seem to like this pose*, she thought as they all smiled at her. *I must do this more often.*

'Wait for us by the Priory porch, Hugh,' said his sister. 'And try not to get into any trouble. Remember the last market day, when you ate an eel pie?'

Hugh screwed up his face. 'I was sick! It was Bernard the baker's fault!'

'You know he gets his meat from the dump outside the walls. I expect all his other food comes from there, too!'

Simone groaned. '*O Dio mio!* Food from the dump!'

'Recycled!' said David, grinning at his cousin. 'Just joking!'

'Let's go now. And look as if we do this every day,' said Tara, adjusting her cap so it covered her hair. 'We can do this. Believe!'

Over the river, across the bridge, and through the old gatehouse they went. Hugh led the horse up the slope to the castle, while the others walked on either side of the cart.

Simone was in a daze. All around her, people

were shouting and laughing. From the quiet of the countryside, she was suddenly in the middle of the town. Market day. It was a hubbub. And the smell! She felt sick. Someone was dumping waste in the river. An alleyway to her right was piled high with rubbish. Was it rotting meat, she wondered, as they made their way up the slope towards the castle. Carts carrying wheat, barley and rye were clattering up alongside them. Some were loaded with firewood. Some had dead game piled up. All were on their way to the castle kitchens.

There were shops to the right and to the left. Ah, cinnamon, she could smell. That was better. Nutmeg, too. The houses were narrow, and, glancing up, she saw someone opening the shutters on the second storey and begin beating a blanket. Dust cascaded down; she coughed and spluttered. '*O Dio mio!*'

'Look at all those beautiful materials,' called Carys as they passed some of the merchants' houses. A large woman was standing nearby, shielding her eyes from the bright sunlight.

'That's Olwyn ap Lewis. She's very wealthy.' Carys turned away, pretending to examine the wheel. 'She mustn't recognise me.'

'Hot pigs' feet! Tasty!' shouted a trader carrying a tray.

'Come! Look at our leather pouches,' called a dark-haired young man standing by a stall. He was smiling at them all.

'Here, take one each. A gift!' He tossed some into the cart.

Simone took one and smiled her thanks, as an older man rushed up and began shouting at him. 'Vincenzo! What are you doing? Why are you giving our wares away to these children? Are you mad?'

'*Ciao! Grazie!*'

'Shush. We don't want to draw any attention to ourselves,' said Tara. 'Let's move on.'

Simone tied the pouch around her neck, and waved to the young man.

'And wisps of hair are escaping from your cap. Tuck them in!' hissed her cousin.

Simone shrugged.

As they arrived at the market cross, they saw an old man in a long brown woollen tunic calling out to the people passing by. 'You have seen the omens in the sky! Soon there will be such terrors across this land. Worse than the plague! Monsters will roam the land. Wars! Death and destruction will befall us! Repent!'

'Why doesn't anyone listen to him?' David asked as they entered the castle courtyard.

They were inside the massive walls; there was the Great Tower, high and strong.

Hugh stopped the cart. 'He says the same thing every market day. And people know it's probably true. But what can we do?' He shrugged. 'We live our lives, we do the best we can.'

'Remember, from now on speak with deep voices.

Or, better – don't speak at all,' whispered Carys to the girls.

David pulled a piece of woollen cloth over Bethan. 'Stay here, and behave.'

The puppy licked his hand and settled down.

'What is this cart doing here? Who are you?'

Tara wheeled around. A grey-haired man with a square, bull-like face was glaring at them. *He's familiar*, she thought. *Chin jutting out, lips curled... he's the man I saw in the Bronze Mirror!*

'That's William Sargeant,' murmured Carys.

He was scowling at Hugh. 'Oh, it's the dead potter's boy. Come to deliver the tiles, have you?'

'Yes, sir.' Hugh lowered his head while Bethan growled under the cloth.

'Unload them, and carry them up to Queen Philippa's chamber.' He waved his arm in the direction of the Tower. 'Not you,' he pointed to Hugh. 'You're a scrawny fellow. You're useless.'

David started to move towards him. How dare he speak to his friend like that? What a bully. Tara pulled him back, but the steward had noticed.

'What are you doing here? You should be with my nephew, preparing for the joust. Tristran!'

A tall boy of about fourteen years of age appeared from behind a stone wall. He looked David up and down as he continued chewing on a leg of chicken. 'Do I know you?'

'You should both be polishing armour. All must be ready for the joust next week, on St Peter and

Paul's Day. And,' the man stared at his nephew, 'you will be serving at the feast tonight. Both of you.'

Tristran smirked at his uncle. 'Come with me, boy. We have much work to do.'

David tried to shake his arm away, and stared at his twin. Tara felt panic rising up inside her. The plan was going wrong already. David was being dragged off to somewhere in the castle. How would they ever find him? What about the will?

Simone moved forwards. 'Dav–'

'Don't do anything, cuz! We'll find him later. Don't show this man that you're afraid. That would be a big mistake. He loves people's fear.'

'Let's unload the cart, and take the tiles up to the Queen's chamber,' called Carys in a deep voice.

'What's your name?' William Sargeant stared at her.

She lowered her eyes. 'Iolo, sir. I'm a neighbour of the Morgans. I've come to help with the tiles, along with our other neighbours.' Carys swept a hand over towards the girls. They kept their eyes on the dusty cobbles.

'Well, I haven't got all day to stand around here. Lord John and Lady Katherine are arriving. There is much to do. When you've completed your job, go to the kitchens. All are needed to prepare for the feast tonight.' The steward turned to Hugh, who was still sitting on the cart. 'Get this cart out of here. Now!'

Hugh flinched. Bethan gave a soft growl.

'And you three... Get those tiles up to the chamber!'

The girls hurriedly took the tiles off the cart, and stacked them by the entrance to the queen's chamber. Simone was soon puffing and panting. As she glanced around, she saw that the steward was still staring at them.

Had he noticed they were girls? She put her shoulders back and strode to the cart to collect more tiles, praying she was moving like a boy.

'Lazy peasants!' muttered the steward. Was there something different about them? He knew most of the people around the Abbey Grange. They didn't look familiar. Were they spies for that Welsh upstart, Glyndwr, trying to get into the castle unnoticed?

Just as he moved towards them, a servant came running up. 'Sir. Lord John and Lady Katherine will be here within the hour. They have made good time from Ross on the Wye.'

William Sargeant halted. He had things to do before his master and mistress arrived. Secret things. Plans to put in place.

'Hurry! Then off to the kitchens!' he shouted, and stalked off towards the Great Hall.

Simone dashed inside the entrance and sat on the stone steps with her head in her hands.

'What are you doing?' Tara asked. 'We have to carry these up, then help Carys to lay them and search for the will.'

'*No!* I don't want to. I'm tired. I'm hot. And I want to go home,' Simone cried. She threw her cap down. 'I hate this thing.' She saw the cart disappearing out of the courtyard. 'And Hugh and Bethan have to leave the castle, and we don't know where David is. Maybe he's been kid– kid–'

'Kidnapped,' Tara sighed. She loved her cousin, but she was definitely hard work. 'No, he's probably fine, sitting in the sun, polishing armour or something, and joking with his new friend, Tristran. We'll meet up with him later.' She was deliberately making light of their situation. But she knew their plan had just been shredded.

Carys had been up and down the narrow stone stairs several times. 'Everything is ready. I've put most of the tiles where they need to go. Can you help me with this last pile?'

Simone jumped up. '*Mi dispiace!* I'm sorry.' She picked up two tiles.

A servant running by stared suspiciously at her.

'Shush, and put your cap back on,' whispered Carys. 'We don't want anyone to know who we are, or why we are here. Remember, be silent, or speak deeply.'

Simone nodded, and raced up the spiral staircase. Tara shook her head. 'She just doesn't seem to realise the danger we are in here.'

Her friend smiled. 'You came to us because you each have a special gift. Together, we'll solve this problem, and all will be well. I believe this.'

All around the castle, the sounds of preparation for the feast grew louder. Servants hurried from the Great Hall to the kitchens and back again, carrying knives and platters, goblets and cloths.

'Make all ready for the arrival of Lord John of Gaunt, and Lady Katherine. Everything must be completed forthwith,' announced a short, dumpy man who was standing in the middle of the courtyard.

'That's Thomas ap Pryce, the clerk,' said Carys. 'He mustn't see me. Let's go up and lay the tiles now. And I have something important to tell you. A secret.'

Chapter 7
In the Queen's Chamber

Tara climbed up the narrow spiral staircase, touching the sides of the thick stone walls as she turned, and turned again, slowly feeling her way. It was gloomy after the brightness of Midsummer's Day. Even the narrow slits of windows let in just a little sunlight. She tried to see outside, but could only get glimpses of the river down below. *Is that the Monnow? These slits must be for the archers to fire their arrows through, at the enemy below.* She shivered.

Carys and Simone were sitting on the floor in the chamber when she arrived.

Red-and-gold tapestries hung on the walls. Cushions were scattered on the window seat that overlooked the gardens.

So this was Queen Philippa's chamber, thought Tara. *Cool.*

'Come and see this pattern,' said Simone. 'Carys's father made these tiles; twenty years ago. *Bellissimo!* The queen loved them!'

Simone had gone to gaze out of the window. 'I might be able to see Lord John and Lady Katherine arriving from here! I wonder what she'll be wearing?'

'A blue and gold gown, with a short ivory veil she had on when I saw her last,' said Carys.

'*Magnifico!* I hope we'll see her.'

Tara was running her fingers over the tiles. 'They are very beautiful. Why did your father choose to make these with animals and birds?'

'He loved all the birds of the river: kingfishers, herons, swans. And he loved animals: beavers, badgers and otters. He designed patterns, too: circles, diamonds, fleur de lys...'

'Look! The pattern – it's like a spiral!'

'At the beginning is a swan.'

'Then a deer. Is that a pig? It's got trees around it.'

'That's a wild boar. There are lots in the forest. The hunters have been out this last month, killing them for the feasts here.'

'Ergh!' said Simone as she looked down at the gardens. 'I so dislike pork.'

'And here's an eel.' Tara touched the image. 'Or could it be a lamprey?'

'There are lots of eels and lampreys in the river. Ah – a coracle with wavy lines. That means a river.'

'What's a coracle?'

'It's a small boat made of willow and animal skin. We use it for fishing on the river. Hugh and I paddle down the river in them. We take one each and hang a net in between. Often, we take home salmon, and other fish, too. Sometimes, we catch lampreys. Coracles are so light, you can easily be caught in the currents and end up back where you started from! Or, if you aren't very good at paddling, you fall in.' She paused. 'Father taught us.'

'Is that how he and your brother drowned?' asked Simone.

Tara shot her a furious look.

'Oh, sorry—'

'That's alright. No, he and James were in a bigger boat, and it overturned by the weir. Perhaps the load was too heavy. Or they may have hit a rock. The river was flowing fast that day. We don't know exactly what happened.' Carys smoothed over the tiles. There was a catch in her voice.

'Could that be a beaver?' asked Tara aloud. *Is it really my job to change the subject when Simone puts her foot in it?* she wondered. *Sensitivity doesn't seem to be her strong point.*

'I'm not sure. But that's definitely a lamprey. It's so ugly. But it tastes good.'

'That one looks like a church, or cathedral, or—'

Simone sat down next to Tara. 'That's an arch.'

'It could be an abbey, or—' said Tara.

'The Priory. Yes! Father made all the tiles for it. And we'll be meeting Hugh there,' said Carys.

'After we've found the will.'

Simone sat back on her heels. 'Can you check with your Mirror where the document is?' she asked. 'That's why we came.'

Her cousin frowned. 'It really doesn't work like that.'

'*Per favore!* Please!'

'I don't want to take it out, in case someone sees it and tries to steal it,' said Tara. 'It is precious, and – magic. It brought us here, but we must work out ourselves what to do.'

Simone glared. 'Why not just look in the Mirror, get the answer, then we can go? *Fini!* Quick! Easy!'

'No.'

'Oh! That was, er – strong – firm.'

'Yes. It was. Otherwise, we'll be going around in circles. Being direct is good.'

Carys touched Tara's arm. 'Hugh and I... we can find where the will is – on our own. We don't want to be–'

'It's fine, Carys. Isn't it, Simone?' Tara gave her cousin The Look.

Simone shrugged. '*Alora!* Do you think we can have a shower while we are here?'

Carys looked puzzled. 'A shower?'

'A wash, a bath? I need to shower every day. It's so hot outside, I'm sure I'll be very smelly very soon.' She wriggled her shoulders. 'Ugh!'

'Rome is hotter than here. Don't worry about it,' said Tara, wishing Simone would stop thinking about herself so much.

Carys smiled, 'When we get home, we can wash our clothes in the stream.'

'Just clothes?'

'Our hands and faces, too. We wash those throughout the day.'

Simone was shocked. 'Have you got any soap?'

'Soap? What's soap?'

'Washing in the stream is fine! Isn't it, cuz?'

The floorboards creaked as Simone jumped up and ran to the door.

'Well, I need to go to the loo. Do they have toilets, privies, in the castle? Lady Katherine won't sit – er, squat – in the bushes!'

Tara groaned.

'I heard when it gets too smelly in one castle, the nobles move to another one,' said Carys. 'That's why the Lord and Lady have come here from Kenilworth.'

'*O Dio mio!*' muttered Simone. 'I have to go to the loo, privy, latrine... whatever you call it. Now.'

'Ask a servant the way,' said Carys. 'But make sure you aren't discovered.'

'And speak in a deep voice,' Tara called after her cousin as she clattered down the winding staircase. *It's no good wishing she was different. She's my cousin, and I love her.*

As she traced the spiral of tiles with her fingers, she whispered, 'From the swan, to the deer, to the boar...'

Came a whisper:

Look and remember, here begins the spiral,
To find its end, you'll travel many a mile.

Carys had gone to the top of the stone steps, and was peering down. There was only silence. She turned back to face her friend, and took a deep breath. 'I've been wanting to tell you something...'

Tara smiled and nodded. 'I know.'

'A huge secret it is.' She paused.

'Shouldn't we wait until we are all together?' Tara knew her twin would hate to be left out.

'Just the beginning, then.' Carys caressed the tiles. 'Father laid these as a – a kind of puzzle – in case he didn't come back.'

'So, this spiral – it's a code?'

'Yes. Look here. Father's mark, his potter's mark, is at the beginning, and at the end. There are three wheels, too. That's the symbol for St Katherine. She's the patron saint of potters.' Carys paused. 'These tiles are at the beginning of the spiral; this first part. And also at the end – look here. He'd never made this pattern before. It must mean something, and these are the only clues left to help us.'

Help us with what, exactly? And clues to what? wondered Tara.

She touched the Mirror, but no whisper came.

'If we remember the birds and animals in the order Father put them, they could reveal the secret...'

They were examining the pattern once more, and memorising the order of the tiles, when they heard footsteps coming slowly up the stairs.

'Listen, someone's coming.'

'Where can we hide?'

'It's only Simone.'

'No,' said Tara. 'These footsteps are heavier.'

'It could be William the steward.'

Thuds came up the staircase; someone was panting.

'Or Thomas the clerk,' added Carys.

A short, dumpy man appeared in the doorway and glowered at the two girls. 'Haven't you finished yet?'

'We were just–' answered Carys in a deep voice.

Tara stared at the man's boots, and swallowed hard.

He glanced around the chamber. 'That will do. This work can be completed when Lady Katherine leaves. She won't be using this room.' He wiped his forehead with a handkerchief. 'You are needed in the kitchens. Go there now!' He turned abruptly, and left the room.

'Thomas ap Pryce. The first Welshman ever to have reached such a high position. Sold his very soul for power and authority, we think.'

'We?'

Carys looked confused for a moment. 'I mean us. Those of us who live around here – in the Marches.'

Tara looked at her new friend. She knew she wasn't telling her everything. Was there yet another secret? There seemed to be layers of them.

'We need to find David,' said Carys quickly. 'And

Simone. She's probably got lost. Let's find the will, and then meet up with Hugh and Bethan at the Priory.'

'But this spiral – the code – the tiles–' began Tara, before she noticed how flustered Carys was. Was it sadness about her father's tiles? Was she frightened about being caught in the castle? Or was it something else?

'Hurry!'

As they rushed down the stairs and out into the sunlight, there was a commotion in the courtyard. A trumpet sounded.

'Wait!' Carys pulled Tara back into the shadows. 'Don't go any further. It must be Lord John and Lady Katherine arriving.'

Tara peeked around the entrance. 'Who are all those people?'

William Sargeant and Thomas ap Pryce were smiling and bowing as the most powerful noble in the land dismounted. He moved slowly and deliberately, handed his reins to a servant, and scanned the castle.

Lady Katherine was smiling at all the people who had come to greet them. Her veil blew gently in the breeze.

'Welcome, Your Grace,' said the steward. 'Your Ladyship. We trust you had a good journey.'

'Coming down from Goodrich was particularly pleasant. The Wye is the most beautiful river. It is good to be back here.' The Lord of the Marches paused. 'Is all quiet? No news of that Glyndwr?'

'All is peaceful, Your Grace. He and his men keep well away.'

'Frightened of Your Lordship, he is,' added Thomas ap Pryce, making a deep bow. Lord John strode past him into the Great Hall.

David had followed Tristran from the courtyard to the back of the castle. Some young boys were polishing armour. When they saw Tristran, they stopped and grinned.

'My uncle is the steward, William Sargeant. He owns a lot of land at Trellech, and he is building a magnificent manor house there,' boasted the young squire as he led David towards the stables. 'His Grace relies on him totally, to keep the Welsh down, keep them in their place, and make sure they keep our laws. He's very good at that.'

'Is he really?' asked David, disliking this boy more and more. He seemed familiar: blue eyes, fair hair, and large, stick-out ears. *I've seen him before,* he thought. *But where? Still, I must work out where I am.*

He glanced around the area, noting where everything was. *Stables here, kitchens over there. I'll need to escape quickly when the time's right.*

And I must find the others soon.

'Here's where I wrestled with Lord John's son, Henry Bolingbroke.' Tristran waved his arms around airily. 'King Richard has just made him Duke of Hereford.'

'Really?' David nodded as he checked all the exits.

'When he's here, we go hunting together. Fishing and jousting, too.'

'Awesome,' he muttered. *So we came in from the courtyard–*

Tristran threw away the chicken bone. 'Of course, Harry – I call him Harry – he's in Ireland presently, with the king. Keeping the peasants down there too, I expect. When he returns, we'll be going hawking together.'

'Great.' David continued to scan the courtyard.

'You're not one of those Glyndwr people?' Tristran stared into his eyes. 'Are you a spy?'

David wasn't sure what to say. He shook his head. "No" seemed to be the safest answer.

'So, who are you?' Tristran picked up a stick, and began making stabbing movements at the ground. 'Who's your father?'

'Sir Benjamin of Burford,' David blurted out, and bit his lip. He felt laughter bubbling up.

Tristran stared. 'I've never heard of him. So – has he sent you here to learn?'

The young time-traveller nodded. 'He has.' That was true enough. He was certainly learning a lot, and his parents had sent him on the dig. At that thought, he suddenly wanted to be back in their new home, by the river.

'Let's get a few things straight. I am in charge here, as my uncle is in charge of the castle. So you do as I say.' The boy put his shoulders back. 'I am the best, so you must be second-best.'

'At what?'

'Everything. Looking after our knight...' He paused. 'Has your father ever taken you to a joust?'

David remembered when he was about six years old, and they had gone to a palace in Oxfordshire to see a medieval joust. 'Yes. It was fun!'

'Fun? *Fun?* Tristran looked shocked. 'See those boys over there, polishing armour? That's what you will be doing all day tomorrow. All day.'

Not if I can escape from here before then, thought David. *I need to distract him.* 'What's that stuffed thing over there?'

'The quintain? You don't know what a quintain is?' Tristran spoke loudly, so the boys could join in his laughter.

'Ah, that's your quintain,' David said hurriedly. 'My eyes were dazzled by the sun glinting on the armour.'

Tristran narrowed his eyes. 'Let's practise our jousting skills on it now. It's very important to get it right.'

'Ah, yes, it is.' David was trying to remember how the quintain worked. He was also suspicious of this arrogant boy.

The young squire strolled over to the pages. He made a comment David couldn't catch, and they looked over, laughing loudly at this new recruit. Just then, a picture came into his head of that joust, and he smiled.

A raven cawed, loud and raspy, from the top of the Great Tower, as David strolled over to the quintain. He grinned at the stuffed mummy-knight, and checked that it was on a swivel.

Tristran and the pages were still laughing as he prodded gently at the clothes on the effigy. It moved towards him: some sand trickled out. David bent down and pretended to brush some mud off his tunic. Picking up a handful of stones, he squeezed them through a hole in the chain-mail. Then he found some bigger stones. Smiling to himself, he thought, *Yes! It's heavier on one side now. Perfect.*

He turned as Tristran swaggered over, holding a long, thick stick.

'Stand aside. I'll show you how it's done. Watch me,' said the young squire, and hit the knight-mummy with all his strength. It swung around, hitting him full and hard in the face. 'Argh! You stinkard! What–!' Tristran fell backwards, screaming and holding his nose. Blood started to drip through his fingers. He glowered at his foe.

Over by the stables, the boys burst out laughing as Tristran ran towards David, tried to punch him, and tripped.

'What did you do? What did you do to the quintain? This is all your fault. I know it is. You've broken my nose. You filthy jackanapes!'

David dodged the blows. His enemy pulled back his fist again, tried to focus, and aimed at his face.

'I didn't do anything,' said David, looking astonished. He tried to smother a grin.

'You did it. I know you did something.' Tristran was trying to staunch the blood from his nose with his left hand, while pawing at the air with his right.

David swerved and missed another punch. 'Can I help you clean up the blood?' he asked. 'I know how to do it. What you have to do is—'

Tristran become even angrier. 'Don't touch me! You must be a spy. I'll tell my uncle to throw you in the dungeons. Stay there. Don't you dare move. I'm going to find him now.'

He called over to the young boys, 'Quiet, you rascals! Make him stay here!' Turning back to David, he spat, 'I'll make you pay for this, son of Sir Benjamin of Burford. And you'll spill everything. Blood and guts!'

He lunged at his enemy once more, but David instantly moved to the right. 'You'll be punished for this.' The young, now blooded, boy, turned away, muttering, 'I'll make sure of it.'

David felt rising panic. *If I'm locked in some dark, dank dungeon, then any hope of meeting up with Tara again and finding a way back to the twenty-first century will be gone. What can I do? What can I say?* He took a deep breath.

'I'm no spy. I've just come here to – to find something,' said David. 'To find something that has been stolen, er… lost… for a long, long time.' He felt something nagging at him in his head. 'Don't tell,' Tara had said. 'Keep *schtum.*'

But this must be different. I can't be locked away. That will ruin everything.

'Find what?' demanded Tristran, as he wiped some blood on his tunic.

David thought quickly. Tell him about the Mirror and the will? Or make up a completely different story? Was he being a coward? Should he just beat up Tristran? He knew he could do it easily, with a couple of jabs to specific places. But it had been many lifetimes since he had done that. He'd learnt the hard way that fighting never solves anything. The Goddess had sent him to Nebula to spend aeons on his own. *I'm not going there again. It was pure hell, and our quest is too important. I'd just feel satisfied with myself for a few minutes. What can I do?*

Avoid. Deflect. Distract, came the whisper.

'I'm here to find something very valuable… very valuable indeed.' David looked Tristran straight in the eyes. 'There was this rich, very rich, knight, who lived near Oxford some time ago. Sir Nicholas. My father knew him well. He and his family had this, well, treasure. Gold, and silver rings, bracelets–'

'Go on.' Tristran dabbed at his nose.

'–necklaces from Europe, gold from the East.'

'Yes, yes. So, where are they?'

He's hooked, thought David. *But what do I say now?*

'Well, one day, Sir Nicholas and his family all caught the plague. When he was dying, he told my father where–'

'Where he had hidden them?'

'Exactly!'

'How could he tell your father, if he had the plague?' asked Tristran, as he tentatively touched his face. Dried blood was caking around his nostrils.

'He called to him through the door of his manor house.' David crossed his fingers, praying his enemy would believe his story. 'He was my father's best friend. It was so sad.' He looked down at the ground. Did this count as telling a lie? He hoped not!

Tristran stared at him. 'I need money to buy armour, and a good horse so I can be a knight. Fight for pride, honour and glory!' He paused. 'Tell me where this treasure is–' the boy's eyes narrowed as he looked away – 'and then we can divide the spoils between us.' He folded his arms.

David knew that that the boy was lying. Eyes down and looking away to the left equals a lie: they'd been taught that on Nebula. Or was it the right? *And now he's folded his arms to cover up his emotions. He wants this so badly, but he isn't sure of me. And he'd double-cross me in an instant.*

Thomas the clerk came waddling towards them.

'You boys!' He waved at the pages by the stables. 'Go to the kitchens now. You're needed there – immediately!' He turned to Tristran. 'You have to go, too. Make sure they are not idle.' Then he noticed David. 'You also.' He looked him up and down. 'You will serve at the high table. The Abbot of Tintern will be there. Make sure your manners are perfect, and your fingernails are clean!' He stared at Tristran. 'And find him a livery collar to wear.'

With that, he moved off towards the Great Tower.

'And so you, my new friend, will do exactly what I tell you to do,' said Tristran, gripping David's arm tightly as he led him off towards the kitchens.

Chapter 8
In the Library

As Simone left the Queen's chamber, she adjusted her cap, making sure any wisps of hair were tucked inside. *This feels so itchy. O Dio mio! Have I got fleas, or maybe lice, or nits? Could I be carrying the plague?* She stopped on the stairs, and touched under her arm. *No boils there. I'll ask Carys what the symptoms are exactly. But I can't think about that now. I must find a loo.*

She dashed down the stairs, and ran out into the sunlight. Dazzled by the sudden glare, she bumped into a young boy carrying some firewood.

'Oh! Er–' She cleared her throat. 'Can you tell me where the toilet is?'

The boy stared at her. A few strands of hair were escaping from her cap.

'Where does Lady Katherine go to use the toilet... the privy? Oh, I have no idea what the word is here.' She looked desperately at the boy and crossed her legs.

He grinned. 'Follow me.' He handed his bundle of

twigs to another servant who was running past. 'Take this to the bakery.'

'Right, Gareth.' The little boy grabbed the kindling, and raced towards the kitchens.

'The bakery! Opposite direction!'

Gareth turned to Simone. 'It's by the Great Hall. Come on.'

They crossed the courtyard to another staircase. Round and round, the girl followed the young boy up the stone steps.

'Here it is.' He looked around. There was no one near. Then he pulled a long, thick curtain aside.

'You'll have to be quick. We're not allowed in here.'

Simone dived behind the tapestry and sat. Heavy footsteps thudded up the stairs.

'What are you doing here? This is not for servants! My lady will be arriving soon. Be off with you!'

Simone froze. Who was this? If she were discovered, she'd be in great trouble.

She could see the tips of leather boots just underneath the thick curtain. She dared not move. She dared not breathe. Light steps scurried away down the spiral staircase.

'Sir! Could you come to the chapel?' a voice called from below. 'The steward would see you urgently.'

A deep sigh. The boots disappeared. Then sounds of weary footsteps going down and down.

Simone counted to sixty. Silence. She peeked

around the curtain. No one was there.

Ergh! That stank! The servants' toilets must be even worse than these. I'm not surprised they died so young. She glanced around. *Which part of the castle am I in?* she wondered. *I must find Tara and Carys – and David.*

She walked along a corridor, down a staircase, and found herself behind a wooden screen. Peeking around it, she saw a vast room with walls covered in rich red-and-gold tapestries.

The Great Hall.

Servants were laying out tablecloths, calling to each other to bring knives, platters, goblets. There were so many entrances and exits. Which part of the castle did they lead to?

O Dio mio! This is a nightmare. How can I find the others? Tara is going to be so mad with me. I know I can be a pain, but if I find the document, that'll make everything all right. Then we can go home. That's if the Mirror can send us home. Will we be stuck here for all eternity? She choked back a sob. *I mustn't cry now. I've a job to do. Dig deep, Simone De Luca Sedky. You can do this. Deep breaths. Now – no eye contact, and look busy. No one will challenge me.*

It was at that moment she noticed William Sargeant standing by the fireplace. Glancing around, he strode swiftly across the Great Hall and slipped out. *That man is the key to this. I know, I'll shadow him.*

'Shoulders back, stand tall,' she murmured. 'Move like a boy. I will be an actor.' She picked up a cloth from a trestle table, and followed the steward.

Outside, she caught sight of him, going into the Great Tower.

Perhaps that's where the will is.

Creeping up the winding staircase, she could hear voices coming from a room at the top. She looked around. There was only another tapestry to hide behind.

If they come out now, they'll discover me. I'll have to slip behind that curtain. These things are so musty and dusty. I might sneeze, and I'll need a story to explain why I'm here. This cloth won't be a good excuse. And perhaps I'll forget my English. O Dio mio! She paused. *Breathe. That's what Tara says. In for two, hold, out for three. Alora! Right. That feels better. I'll say I've come to find him, to ask him something. Er – where are the gardens? I need to find My Lady Katherine. Something like that.*

She tiptoed up, around, and reached the top of the stairs. There was a door to the left; another to the right was slightly open. Quiet voices. Simone could just hear it was the steward and his clerk. She moved nearer.

'Does your assistant suspect anything?'

'I hope not. I showed him the Lord's seal. It looks authentic.'

'What happened to the man who made it?'

There was a pause. 'Rest assured. He's gone away. For a long time.'

Simone caught her breath. Was this even more serious than stealing some land?

'And the documents?'

'I hid them in the library. It's only used when Lord John and Lady Katherine come here.'

'Where exactly, Thomas?'

A hesitation. 'Between the Latin and the Romance books. There's a wooden chest that hasn't been opened for many years.'

'Is it locked? Where's the key?'

'Lost,' Thomas said hurriedly. 'But it matters not. I've covered the important documents with some old manuscripts. Hardly anyone reads Latin, or indeed anything else. They won't know what they're looking at.'

'True. True. But when Henry Bolingbroke comes back from Ireland, he'll be in there. We all know how he loved to read to his late wife. And it would be a disaster for us if he, or any of that family, finds these documents. You do know how dangerous this is...?'

Simone inched towards the door.

'Shall I move them today?'

'No, wait. There's the feast and the joust. Do it after...'

Their voices dropped lower. Simone leaned further forward, to catch their words.

'So Lord John is ailing, and King Richard would like his son, Henry, to, shall we say, move on? Go into exile? Or something else?'

'Careful.' A pause. 'Can I trust you, Thomas?'

'Completely, sir.'

'I have been told... the king is keen for him to – er – disappear. When his father dies, Henry will inherit everything. Henry Bolingbroke, Henry of Derby, and now Henry of Hereford, too! After Lord John dies, he will be Lord of the Marches. So many titles! So much wealth! He will be the most powerful noble in England and Wales. Richard desires his lands, particularly these here in the Borderlands.'

'But–'

'He is the king, Thomas. Richard can do anything he wishes to. However, as we know, Henry Bolingbroke is fiery.'

'Yet the people love him.

'Not the king.'

'No, they believe him to be a tyrant.'

'Shush! I have heard it said, Thomas, that the king will connive at sending Henry into exile in France, or... there could be an accident...' A pause. 'In September, there will be a joust in Coventry, between Henry and...'

Simone was trying to understand. *Connive? Oh, my rusty English. They said the king is plotting against the lord of this castle. That's John of Gaunt. To kill him? Or his son, Henry? Or both?*

What should I do? Who should I tell? How will they do these things? A dagger in the back? Poison? This is an assassination! O Dio mio!'

Floorboards creaked. The oak door began to open wide.

Diving behind the tapestry, Simone pressed her back flat against the stone wall. She prayed that the men would not discover her there. The curtain rubbed against her nose. Dust.

I must not sneeze. I must not, she prayed. Just inside her nostrils, she could feel the itchiness starting. She slowly moved her hand up to her face, and pinched her nose.

Thomas was walking past her. 'We have chosen the right side, haven't we? We are living in such uncertain times.'

'John of Gaunt is old, and he is sick. It will be merciful to help him on his way, Thomas. Then we will be in favour with the king. He will do what he likes with Henry. Ah – I will be richly rewarded. My new manor at Trellech will be magnificent.'

As the two plotters walked down the stairs, the steward said, 'After this, you can go back to Powys, Thomas. Or wherever it is you come from. Be with your own people.'

'No, I – I do not want to return there. Never! You know my people still endure the harsh laws of Edward I. If I lived there, my life would be – it would not be as comfortable as it is here.'

'Ah, no...'

'And I would be made to join Glyndwr and fight the king. Please don't send me back.'

'Thomas! Thomas! I was jesting! Ah, your compatriots would prefer to die fighting us, rather than die in their beds! No, I understand that taking up arms is not for you. People may call you a coward, of course. I have heard it said that you have sold your soul to the English. But stay! Yes, do! Stay here in the Welsh Marches, and reap the rewards of your...'

The sound of their footsteps died away. Simone pushed the tapestry aside, sneezed loudly twice, ran into the room, and closed the door behind her.

She sat on a window seat and gazed down at the river. Branches of willows billowed in the breeze. A gleam of gold, a flitter of bright wings. *What bird is that? I must ask Hugh.* She shook herself.

The will! I must go to the library, and search in that chest. But there'll be all kinds of parchments in there. She sighed. *I wish the twins and Carys were here. Should I go and find them? Or should I go to the library? How will I know which is the right document?*

She held out her hands, and weighed the two choices. Tara or the library? Seconds passed... a minute. She stared at her palms. *If I had the Bronze Mirror, it could tell me. I can't go back empty-handed. Make a decision.*

She stood up. The library. *It won't take long.* She tucked her hair carefully into the cap, pushed back her shoulders, and went down the stairs to the courtyard. Gareth was carrying pails of water towards the kitchens.

'You again. You nearly got me into trouble.'

'I just need to know where the library is.'

'Why? Are you a thief?'

'*No!* I like to read books, that's all.'

Gareth was astonished. 'Read? You? Those books – in the library – they are worth a lot of money. And they're in Latin. Only monks and priests read that language.'

Latin! Yes! thought Simone. *Close to Italian. That could work.*

'I love reading books in Latin.' She smiled at the boy, and lowered her eyes. 'I'm thinking of becoming a monk.'

Gareth stared at her, then shrugged. 'I sometimes see Lady Katherine sitting in the herb garden by the river, reading a book with her ladies.'

'Exactly. She has asked me to go and choose a few books for her.'

The boy continued to look suspicious.

She deepened her voice. 'So she can read them while the knights are preparing for the joust.'

Would that work? She crossed her fingers.

'Go to the West Tower over there, and open the first door. The chapel is on the right, the library is on the left. Be careful with the door. It's very heavy.'

Simone smiled her thanks, strode off across the courtyard, and stood in front of the huge oak door. She twisted and tugged at the black iron handle. It would not move an inch. She pulled again; it moved a little. 'Once more,' she muttered. 'Heave.' The door creaked, and she slipped through the narrow opening.

'*O Dio mio!*' The room was vast. Leatherbound books were stacked from floor to ceiling, shelves and shelves of them. A wooden stepladder leant against the fireplace.

I hope I don't have to climb up to the top shelf to search for these documents, she thought. *No, wait. He said they were in a chest. Between Latin and Romance.*

Her stomach began to rumble. It had been a long time since she had eaten anything. A couple of cheese and tomato sandwiches at the well, a few crumbs of stale bread at the cottage. *How I'd love the biggest plate of lasagne ever now, this minute. But first I have to search for the will.*

Glancing around, she noticed a wooden chest under an arched window.

'This must be it,' she murmured, as she ran her fingers over the curved top. '*Bellissimo!* It's so beautiful.'

Putting both hands underneath the lid, she tried to lift it up, but it wouldn't move. Had Thomas lied? *Is it locked?* She sighed. So many secrets.

Where would he hide the key?

Quills, an inkwell, and some sheets of parchment were lying on top on a small writing desk over by the fireplace. Two drawers were on either side.

Is it in one of those?

Simone slid the left one open. A quill-sharpener. She tried the other one. A long piece of blue silk scrunched up in a corner. As she took it out, something fell to the floor. A black metal key. So Thomas had lied to his master. Why? *No one trusts anyone here.*

Throwing the silk over a chair, she ran to the chest and turned the key in the lock. Nothing. She tried again. A click. She lifted the lid, and peered inside. It was crammed full of rolls and rolls of parchments. She picked some up and stared at them for several minutes, feeling hopeless.

How am I going to know which is the right will? Thomas said that some of these documents are fake. She knelt down and began rifling through them all. *Here are some seals, too. Perhaps these are fake. If I take a couple with me now, we can show them to Lord John and Lady Katherine, and prove these men are not only thieves and forgers, but they are plotting against them, too. We can tell them his son is in great danger. They'll have to believe us.*

She snatched up several of the smaller parchments, a couple of seals, and stuffed them inside her leather pouch. Then she tied it around her neck again and hid it beneath her tunic.

But where is the will? Is it here? Or in the cellar under the Great Hall?

She took a deep breath, and once more searched through the contents of the chest. One document caught her eye: **Owen ap Morgan.**

That was their father's name. It says "Trellech". This is it! This is the will! I've found it! Bravo, Simone! But – O Dio mio! It's in medieval Latin. Some words are familiar. Others... I can't make them out. But this has to be the will. Si! It will prove Eva and the family own their land. She picked up another document that looked similar.

Could this be the fake one? Is this John of Gaunt's seal or not?

She folded them both inside a red leatherbound book and placed it on the desk.

Maybe there are other things, important things, here, she thought. As she scrabbled around the bottom of the chest, she noticed a gold brooch of a white swan, some gold rings, and silver necklaces, too.

These look valuable. But if I take them with me, they'll accuse me of stealing.

She sat back on her heels, and thought for a moment. *I could find a way to speak to Lady Katherine, to tell her about this jewellery.*

Simone was just locking the chest when the library door opened.

Startled, she jumped up. The key dropped onto the floor.

'Who are you? What are you doing?' Thomas waddled towards her, arms outstretched, ready to stop her escaping.

Simone kicked the key under the desk, snatched the book, caught up the piece of silk, and wrapped it tightly around her.

Then, shaking off her cap, she turned to face the clerk and curtsied. '*Mi dispiace.* Pardon me, sir. Noble sir. My lady, she ask me to look for book. To read. In the garden. But—' She rolled her eyes and shrugged. 'Nothing...'

She smiled at the squat little man.

'Oh. I understand.' He frowned, not knowing whether to believe her.

'Yes, yes, go to my lady. Good. Good.'

Simone walked regally to the door, without a glance at him. Then, as she reached the top of the stairs, she hurtled down, singing to herself, 'I found it! I have it!' She halted at the bottom, murmuring, 'Now I must find Tara and Carys. And David. Where is he?'

☆☆
☆ Chapter 9
At the Feast

'Stand here, and don't move!' said Tristran, as he felt his blooded nose. 'Ouch!'

David gazed around. They were standing in the middle of a huge kitchen. Servants were cutting up carcasses, or filleting fish. Others were running backwards and forwards, carrying dishes: meatballs in jelly, boiled venison, and chicken and pork in breadcrumbs.

He grinned. *So*, he thought, *they liked chicken nuggets in 1398, too.*

Tristran prodded him in the ribs.

'Hey! I need to tell my uncle about the treasure. You will have to reveal everything, otherwise we'll throw you into the dungeons. And there you will stay and rot!'

Thomas appeared in the doorway. 'Tristran, where is that girl?'

'What girl? I haven't seen a girl. I'm looking for my uncle.'

Thomas peered at his face. 'Has something

happened to your nose?' He flicked his wrist. 'It is of no matter. Make sure no blood goes into the food.'

Tristran glowered at him. 'Blockhead,' he muttered.

David kept his eyes lowered while Thomas walked around, peering into the various dishes. 'Ah, mortrews! And beavers' tails,' smiled the clerk. 'A favourite of mine. What an enticing aroma! A splendid feast this will be!' He walked out, swinging his hips from side to side.

He likes his food, thought David. *So do I. But beaver tails – yuk! Horrendous!*

He sniffed. *Still, these smells are amazing... fresh bread. And that must be fish – herring, salmon? Tantalising! And I am starving.* He glanced over at a number of pots simmering above the fire.

'Keep your eyes to yourself,' snapped Tristran. 'Wash your hands, then chop those leeks.'

'You know nothing, boy! Nothing!' shouted the chef, rushing over to Tristran. 'I told you, never again will you come into my kitchens. You are a bespoiler! I don't want your spit in my dishes! Go to the Great Hall. Make yourself useful there!'

The young squire scowled, and hissed under his breath to David, 'I'll get you later.'

'Here, boy, chop up this parsley,' said the chef. 'Then mix it with this spinach. It's a special dish for the Abbot of Tintern. He is very partial to it. A weak stomach, he says.' The chef smiled. 'But he also enjoys these lampreys, in a particularly wonderful beef sauce. So beautifully red. Green spinach and red fish. Oh, the colours!' And he kissed his fingertips. 'Magnificent!'

He waved his hand towards a scrawny lad standing by a simmering pot. 'You!' he called. 'Stir those beaver tails!' Then, poking his new servant in the back, he said, 'Parsley! Chop! Now!'

David grabbed a knife, and frantically chopped the herb. *I need a good escape route*, he thought, as he glanced around the kitchens. A few boys near the fire were carving the different meats. One young lad came in, carrying a squawking chicken.

'Take it outside and wring its neck!' shouted the chef. 'Prepare the boar!' he called to another servant. And, to a third, 'Dismember that heron properly this time. Lord John is very particular. As am I!'

A few hours later, the feast was ready. David had run up and down the cellar stairs, carrying wine. He had churned cheese, carved wild boar into slices, and turned a lamb over the fire. 'I am so roasted!' he muttered.

Tired, hot and sweaty, he leant up against the stone wall and sighed. *Why have I been chosen to serve Lord John, Lady Katherine and the Abbot at the high table? And with Tristran?*

'What do I have to do at the feast?' David asked the chef.

Never will I offer to help in the kitchen again. This is like being on a Cook-Off TV programme, only worse, he thought.

An image of his parents busy unpacking in their new home by the river flashed into his mind. He wiped away drops of sweat from his face, and wished he were there.

'Follow that boy Tristran's instructions,' said the chef. 'At least he has learnt the manners required. Just don't stare or look around you. Or pick your fingernails. Or indeed anything else.'

David nodded. *Tristran really wants to get me in trouble*, he thought. *This is going to be a nightmare. Do something wrong, or forget to offer a dish to the right person in the right order, and I could be thrown in the dungeons. Help! Someone help me!*

'So, that's what I heard when I was standing outside the door,' said Simone. She had found Tara and Carys huddled together at the back of the chapel. 'What are you doing here?'

'Hiding,' said her cousin. 'Thomas ordered us to the kitchens, so we are staying here for a while. Have you seen David?'

'No, but I've found something.' Simone walked to

the front of the chapel and swivelled around. *I am going on the stage. Or maybe the movies.* She smiled at the girls, and held up the leatherbound book. 'Very special. And very important.'

'The will! You've found the will!'

'Oh, you are brilliant, cuz.'

They rushed down the aisle.

'I know!' The young girl gave one document to Carys. 'That's the real one; your father's will. For you and your family.' She then gave one to Tara. To her cousin, she said, 'I think that's the fake one. The vellum is different, and the ink, too. We'll have to show them both to Lord John.'

'Thank you, Simone. *Diolch. Diolch.* How can I ever show my gratitude to you?' Carys pointed at the document. 'There's our family name. That's Father's mark.'

Tara hugged her cousin. 'Well done, you.'

Simone looked pleased. 'It was difficult to understand all of it, because it was in medieval Latin. Er, I mean, the Latin of this time. But it is your father's will, Carys. It is your land. Here. Look.' She placed her finger where it was written: "Owen ap Morgan".

'Now you have to present it to Lord John,' said Tara.

Carys was terrified. 'Oh! I can't–'

'We'll help you – won't we, Simone?'

Up in the gallery, the three girls gazed down at the goings-on in the Great Hall. Below them, they could see the servants bringing in platters of roast beef, baby rabbit, pigeon, and stewed swan. There were fish dishes, too: salmon and trout, perch in jelly, and lampreys from the river.

At the north entrance stood William Sargeant, giving orders to the servants. Lord John, Lady Katherine and their guests were seated at the high table, talking and laughing as the feast began.

A group of musicians at the opposite end of the Great Hall were entertaining the guests. Some were playing bagpipes and recorders, one was strumming a harp, and a young boy was singing a merry tune.

'Wow! This all sounds amazing!' said Tara. 'What are those instruments?'

'That's a shawm, and that man over there has a citole.' Her friend sighed. 'I wish Hugh was here. I wonder what he's doing.'

'Playing his whistle by the river with Bethan,' said Simone. 'Look! There's David!'

They craned their necks further over the wooden balustrade. A boy with dark hair in the livery of John of Gaunt was carrying a huge dish, and leading a procession of servants towards the high table.

'What's that on his dish?' asked Simone.

'A peacock. It's an important symbol for his lordship,' said Carys.

'*O Dio mio!* They eat peacocks!' Simone screwed her face up. '*Disgusto!* Horrible!'

Tara nudged her. 'Remember, different times, different tastes.'

'Oh no!' said Carys. 'Look! What's he doing? This is terrible!'

The girls stared in horror. Tristran was about to put his foot out and trip up David as he moved nearer to the high table. He would be sent sprawling. She sent him a mind-message. *Danger! Avoid his foot!*

David instantly moved sideways, placed the dish in front of Lord John, and bowed deeply. A trenchard with fish in a red sauce was set down next to the dish.

'A splendid peacock, Lord John!' exclaimed an old man dressed in white-and-black robes.

'Try some of this lamprey, Father Michael. It will go well with the dish of spinach.'

'Your Grace is most kind,' said the abbot. He took a large portion of the fish, and put it on his platter. 'You were saying about the burning of your palace, the Savoy. A terrible business.'

'It was. Some time ago now, of course. But the peasants were determined to raze it to the ground. They crushed all the jewels they could find underfoot One tried to steal a chalice, but the others flung him on the fire. "Don't steal," the peasants shouted. Astonishing!'

'A bad business,' agreed the abbot. 'They'll all burn in Hell.'

Tara saw her twin move towards the monk, with a flask of wine.

Don't pour it over him, David. She sent him another mind-message. *We have other battles to win! And they have—*

— their beliefs. I know.'

He filled the abbot's goblet.

And don't wish it chokes him!

Can we leave soon, Twin?

We have to wait until after the last course. You'll see why. Be ready.

All around the Great Hall was gossip and laughter, as the guests enjoyed the variety of wines and dishes.

Carys whispered, 'The feast must be coming to an end. They're bringing in the fruit and bread.'

The musicians, along with the acrobats and jugglers, were preparing to leave.

Came a whisper from the Mirror:

The time has come. The girl will speak.

She must have courage. She must not be weak.

Tara put her arm around her friend. 'Go down now, and make your request to Lord John.'

The young Welsh girl started to tremble.

'Or Lady Katherine,' added Simone. 'She looks kind. Go on.'

'What shall I say? She may tell William the steward to throw me out.' Carys gripped her friend's arm. 'You take the will and speak to him. Or Simone–'

Shaking her head, Tara said, 'No. You have to do this yourself. But we'll come with you.'

Simone hugged Carys. 'You can do it, like we practised. Bow, hand her your father's real will–'

'Then explain there's been a misunderstanding. This document is genuine – it shows that your family is entitled to stay on that land at Trellech.'

'A misunderstanding?' said her cousin. '*No!* It's fraud! Deception!'

'Let's try to settle this quietly, and try not to cause a massive argument.' Tara turned to Carys. 'You need to do this for your mother and your family. Believe in yourself. Have courage.'

'Stand up straight, too. After you've bowed.'

'Yes, thank you, Simone. Look at her directly, but with great respect, offer her the document, and say clearly, "This is my father's will. It proves this land at Trellech belongs to my mother, Eva ap Morgan, and my family."'

'I–' Carys hesitated.

'Imagine you are a princess, and expect her to say yes–'

'And she will,' added Tara as she touched the Mirror in her bag. 'She will.'

The girls crept down the stairs from the gallery, slipped into the Great Hall, and hid behind the wooden screen. David was standing behind the abbot with a folded cloth, staring at the roast venison.

'Have you had more work carried out at Tintern – at the Abbey – this year?'

The abbot nodded. 'Yes, my lord. The floor of my new apartments needed tiling, so the potter from Trellech was going to bring them with his son. However, a few days before, their boat capsized by the weir, and they were both drowned. Only one body has been found so far. A most unfortunate business. And inconvenient, too. We will have to engage another potter now.' He took a sip of wine. 'And Owen ap Morgan, he was an excellent craftsman.'

'Is that unusual – for a drowning so near the Abbey?'

The abbot looked away. 'After the spring tides, the weirs were altered. It was all to do with a dispute between the Gloucestershire side and the Welsh side. I imagine that may have led to the accident.' As he reached for some more fish, he said, 'From what I heard, he didn't leave a will.'

David bent down to whisper in the abbot's ear,

'But he...'

The monk had turned to see who was speaking when Tristran kicked David in the back of his knees. He staggered, dropped his cloth, and stood up straight. The steward rushed over, to see what was happening.

'Pick up that cloth,' he hissed.

'Uncle,' muttered Tristran. 'I must tell you – this boy knows where some treasure is. We must make him talk. Shall we throw him in the dungeons?'

'What are you talking about? Be quiet. Remember where you are.' He bowed deeply to Lord John, who had raised an eyebrow.

'Making sure all is well, Your Grace.' He turned to his nephew and snarled, 'You know nothing.' Then he smiled at his master and said, 'Beg pardon. A slight mishap.'

It was at this point that Tara gave Carys a little push.

The girl took a deep breath, and walked slowly up the Great Hall, towards the high table. Taking off her cap, she curtsied to Lady Katherine and said, 'My Lady, er – your ladyship. May I beg a few moments of your time?'

'A girl!' The steward was taken aback. How could he have missed her? What was she doing in there? Then he recognised her. 'The potter's daughter!' Fear gripped him.

He rushed over and bowed to Lady Katherine. 'I'm sorry, my lady. I don't know how this – this person – could have entered here. A peasant...'

Swivelling around, he whispered to Carys, 'Get out! Leave now. Do not trouble her ladyship, or–'

'No, I'll not leave. It is my right.' Carys raised her voice. 'My Lady, I am not a peasant. I am free-born. My family and I, we have land near Trellech. My father was Owen ap Morgan; a craftsman, a potter, renowned for his beautiful tiles all over the Welsh Marches. And here, in Queen Philippa's chamber, in the Priory church, and–' She waved her hand towards the monk – 'in the Abbey, too. My father, Owen, and elder brother, James, drowned at the weir near Tintern. The level of the weirs had been changed.' She stared at the abbot. 'Then your steward, William Sargeant, and his clerk, Thomas ap Pryce, came to Trellech, to our home, and showed us a document. We had never seen it before.'

Carys choked back the emotions that began to well up. 'They–' She struggled to speak.

Lady Katherine smiled encouragingly. 'Go on, my dear. What was this document?'

Carys looked directly into her eyes; eyes full of kindness. She took a deep breath. 'It was written in Latin, so we, the family, could not understand it. The steward told us that because Father had died, our land now belonged to his Lordship. That is the law, he said, and waved it at my mother.'

Carys knew that the Lord of the Marches was listening intently. She could feel his piercing eyes on her. 'Your Ladyship, my mother knew – we knew – that Father had left everything to us, to his family. He had made a will. Here it is.' She held it up in her right hand. 'Father's mark is on it. It is genuine.'

The steward shook his head frantically. 'No. No. That's not...'

Then Carys held up the second parchment. 'However, this document – the one the steward showed us – this says our land belongs to Lord John, and it looks as if his lordship's seal is fixed to it–' she paused – 'but it has been forged!'

There was a gasp around the Great Hall.

'That day, William Sargeant announced that Lord John now owns our home, our land, our kilns, all we possess. And we must leave on St Peter and St Paul's Day. We will be destitute, My Lady. But see–' Carys held up the will – 'this document is truly my father's will. It has his seal.' She bowed. 'May I therefore request a – a *quitclaim*?'

Lady Katherine stared long and hard at the steward. 'This is a peculiar business.'

'The girl doesn't understand, your ladyship.' His voice cracked. 'She's confused. She said herself that she cannot read. It is really nothing to do with forged documents or a *quitclaim*.'

Carys glared at him. 'I can read English and Welsh. I said I cannot read Latin. But my friend here can.' She pointed towards Simone.

'She has no proof–' The steward clasped and unclasped his hands.

Carys held up the genuine document. 'This is the legal will,' she said firmly. She placed it on the table in front of Lady Katherine. Then she held up the second document. 'This is fake!'

There was a groan from the steward.

'It has the seal of the Lord of the Marches, but it has been forged.' Carys pointed to William Sargeant. 'He desires our land, and steals the land of others by foul means – to increase his wealth.' She paused. 'And there is more, my lady; he is plotting with the king against Lord John and his son, Henry Bolingbroke. The king intends to send him into exile or have him killed in an accident. Simone, my friend here, heard him telling his clerk, Thomas ap Pryce. I too overhead them when they came to Trellech that day.'

The steward was holding his head in his hands. 'Oh no! No!'

'And poison was spoken of...'

At that point, Thomas the clerk came rushing forward. 'All this is true, my lady. He revealed this plot to me. I was waiting for the right time...' He bowed deeply.

William Sargeant froze. 'Your Grace, I-I... These are all lies!' He looked wildly around the Great Hall. There was only a deep, shocked silence.

Simone stepped forward and curtsied. 'All this is true, my lady. I was in the library. I looked in the chest, and these documents were hidden there. At the bottom of it, I saw a gold brooch – it had a white swan on it. There were some rings, and other jewellery, too.' She pointed to the clerk. 'He had hidden them.'

Lady Katherine murmured, 'Mary's brooch. We had thought it lost...'

Tristran slipped out of the north entrance, just as his uncle and the clerk found themselves standing before Lord John of Gaunt, Lord of the Marches, accused of theft, forgery and plotting against him.

'Betrayal! Thievery!'

A gesture. Lord John's men surrounded the terrified miscreants.

William Sargeant continued to protest. 'Lies! Lies! And my nephew has just told me that boy–' he pointed at David '–told him of some lost treasure. Gold, silver. He's been searching for it in this castle. He's a spy. They are spies... For the king, for Glyndwr...' He kept babbling as the knights held him. 'Tristran will tell you – he knows. We can share the treasure...'

Above the shouting and commotion, Carys heard Lady Katherine say, 'You are a brave young woman. Leave the matter of this *quitclaim* with me. I will look into it.' With that, she glided out of the Great Hall.

Came the whisper from the Mirror:

Go quickly. Leave this place
To the Priory make haste
Wait there in the shadows

For you must not be traced.

Pandemonium had broken out. The steward was shouting at Thomas. The clerk was weeping.

A command was given: 'Take them to the dungeons.'

Tara caught hold of Carys and Simone. 'The Priory. Now!'

David began edging along the high table towards them.

'Which way, Carys?' asked Tara.

'Follow me.'

'Hurry, Twin!'

The clamour in the Great Hall could still be heard as they hurtled across the courtyard and out through the castle gates.

None of them noticed a figure hugging the walls; staying in the shadows; keeping his distance, as they raced along the winding alleyways and through the Priory gardens.

☆☆
☆ **Chapter 10**
At the Priory

Carys arrived first, and breathless, at the Priory, to find Hugh sitting by the porch gate, eating a pasty. Bethan was staring up at it.

'I left the cart with–' said Hugh, as he tried to swallow his mouthful all in one go.

'Run! Run into the church! Lord John's men might be chasing us.'

'Why–?' Hugh choked and dropped the pasty on the ground. The puppy devoured it instantly.

'That was my eel pasty!'

'You were sick the last time you ate one,' said Carys, as she ran up the path towards the church door.

'Where are the others?'

The twins and Simone arrived, also out of breath. Bethan jumped up, barked, and wagged her tail furiously.

'I think Lord John's men went down to the town,' said David, fussing the spaniel.

'But why chase us?' asked Simone. 'We haven't

done anything wrong.'

'No. But all this will take time to settle down. And we have things to do,' said Tara.

'Let's go in,' said Carys, pulling open the thick oak door. The air inside the church felt cool. 'We can hide in one of the side chapels until we know we are safe.'

'You'll have to be quiet, Bethan,' said David, stroking the puppy's head. She nuzzled his leg.

'Have you seen anyone around here, Hugh?'

'No, no one has passed by.'

Carys led the way down the main aisle. It was quiet and gloomy in the church. Only the red light of the altar lamp glowed.

The girl turned off to a small side chapel on the left. They all shuffled into the wooden pews, and sat in silence for a few minutes.

'We'll be safe here. They can't drag us out,' said Hugh. 'We're in sanctuary. It's holy,' he explained.

'In Italy, we've lots of sanctuary – in the churches.' Simone frowned at the boy.

Tara smiled. She'd noticed how annoyed her cousin got when people explained things to her, especially when she already knew them.

'But Lord John's men only have to wait for us to come out,' said David. 'And a priest might see us...'

Hugh grinned. 'The abbot is in Rome. I heard that at the market. Father Bernard has gone off to another monastery, to copy a manuscript for the library. He'll be away for months. And no monks are here to help the sick.' He paused. 'I had an adventure while you were in the castle.' He looked sideways at his sister.

'You can tell us about it later,' said Carys, remembering all the other times Hugh had got into trouble at the market. Once she'd had to get him out of the stocks before he got pelted with rotten fish.

'*Alora!* Lady Katherine has the will. *Fini!* It's finished. We can go home now.' Simone stared at Tara. 'Can't we?'

'You've found the will?' said David. 'Cosmic!'

'Where is it?' asked Hugh.

Carys told them about all that had happened in the castle, that she had given the document to Lady Katherine, and had asked for a *quitclaim.*

'And William Sargeant and Thomas ap Pryce have been taken to the dungeons.'

David grinned. 'If we'd stayed longer, I could've taken part in a joust. I'd have liked that.'

'Tristran would have wounded you. He'd have made sure of that. You've made an enemy there,' said Tara, adding under her breath, 'For ever...'

'Bethan will protect me,' laughed David, as the puppy put her head on his lap.

'Shall we tell them about the other thing now?' Hugh asked his sister. 'The secret?'

David opened his eyes wide. 'A secret? Another one?'

'I'm sorry,' said Carys. 'We had to find the will

first. You see – finding it was only the first part.'

Simone sighed deeply. There was more to do before they could go home.

David mind-messaged his sister. *Part of what? Why haven't you told us this before?*

I only found out a bit about it when we were in Queen Philippa's chamber. I said let's wait till we were all together. There's no need to be cross, Twin.

'Can you tell us the secret now then, Carys?'

The brother and sister stood on the step by the altar rail, and faced their friends.

'This secret has been in our family for nearly two decades,' began the young girl.

'Monumental!' said David.

'It's a kind of puzzle – a code...'

'About a casket,' added Hugh.

'A casket?' said Simone. 'For a dead body?'

Carys looked confused. 'No. A box; a precious box.'

'Maybe it'll have something important in it,' said her brother.

'Treasure!' murmured David. 'Oh, this is exciting!'

Tara thought she heard a movement outside the Priory. 'Shush, a minute.'

They held their breaths. Was there someone listening?

A branch scratched against the stained-glass window. Silence.

'Only the wind,' said David. 'Go on. We're in suspense.' He glanced at Simone. 'Well, I am!'

His cousin rolled her eyes, and looked up to the arched ceiling.

Carys hesitated, then continued their story. 'The day before he drowned, Father told us he'd taken some tiles down the valley to Tintern Abbey, and was on his way home when he saw a stranger by the mill. Dressed in rags, he kept looking up and down the path, in a wild kind of way. Then he collapsed. Father lifted him onto the cart, and took him to the Abbey. He knew Brother Luke would care for him in the infirmary there. For days, Father sat with him after his work, while the monks were praying, or fishing, or beekeeping—'

'—or telling people not to go on pilgrimages, just to give money to the monks instead,' said Hugh. 'They like wealth.'

Simone nodded. 'That's true.'

'This man, Edward, he was from London, but he had left there for Bristol. He was sick, and believed he was dying. He had a high fever, and sometimes his words, his ideas, were all mixed up.'

Hugh carried on. 'Then one evening he was calling out, shouting. He caught hold of Father's sleeve and told him he had a great secret. "I beg you, tell it to the abbot. Confess to him," said Father. "I am not a priest." "No, no. This abbey is rich. It has lands, treasures. This abbot is powerful, close to John of Gaunt. I will tell you, only you." He whispered this secret: "Some years ago, 1381 it was, my wife and I, along with Wat Tyler and thousands of people, men and women, we began a rebellion against the Lord Chancellor and the lawyers. They were oppressing us. The poll tax they had imposed on us all was a shilling a head. A shilling! And for what? To pay for the long war with France. We were suffering terribly. Men in their thousands dying across the water. And for what? Nothing! Wars! All wars are pointless. It is always the innocent who suffer." His voice became croaky; it was difficult for him to speak. Father gave him sips of water. "But in the end, there was violence. Not one of us had wanted that. We'd rebelled so we would get justice from the king. That was what the people were asking for... Justice..."'

Hugh nodded towards his sister.

She continued the story: "'We asked," he said, "that the young King Richard listen to our pleas. We wanted freedom. Freedom from the lords. An end to corruption. Freedom to rent or buy land, to buy and sell goods at market. Equality. So many things were promised then... so many things. Promises made, promises broken." His breath became shallow, but he was determined to tell all this to Father.'

Hugh took up the tale: 'Edward said, "We went to Lord John of Gaunt's palace: the Savoy Palace. White and beautiful. So much wealth: rich tapestries, gold and silver plate. When we saw it, we wanted to destroy it: we didn't want to steal anything. 'Truth, freedom, justice!' we shouted. Then we threw the plate into the river, smashed the jewels into tiny bits with our axes, and stamped on the gems until they were dust. Some tore down the tapestries; others ripped cushions and silk hangings, and made a fire in the middle of the Great Hall. Others went to the cellars, and began drinking wine. There, they found some barrels, and, thinking they were full of gold, threw them on the fire. But there was an almighty explosion. What an explosion! It wasn't treasure, it was gunpowder. Such chaos and confusion followed. And death! Death!'"

'I know!' David broke in. 'Someone tried to steal a gold plate, or a chalice, and the others threw him into the fire.' He felt his sister was frowning at him. 'I heard Lord John telling the abbot at the feast.'

Carys nodded. 'Edward said it was terrible. Such anger. Such hate. And for what? Nothing. Nothing came of this rebellion, not at that time.'

'What happened then?' asked Simone, leaning forward.

Hugh continued: 'The fire was raging, the walls were falling down. Edward heard the men in the cellar screaming; they were trapped. It was then he turned and saw this casket. Blue and gold, with a peacock on it. It was so beautiful. He took it. He stole it. Since that moment, he told Father, his life had been cursed.'

Simone threw up her hands. 'What did I say? *O Dio mio!* There's a curse!'

'Edward's breath was slow and painful, but he was determined to finish his story,' said Carys. 'He had a spasm of coughing, then said, "I have come to this place, to these lands of John of Gaunt, to return this casket to him, but in secret. If he knew of this, I would surely be hanged. But it matters not now. I am dying. Perhaps I have brought the plague here. It is rife in Bristol. So many are dying there. Cursed, I surely am. Find the casket. Return it to Lord John, I beg you. Promise me this. Then I can die in peace."'

Hugh added, 'Father gave his word, but his mind was in turmoil. He was scared, thinking he might have caught the plague from Edward. He knew young men in nearby Caldicot who had caught the disease; many had died. Monks in the Abbey, too. But his greatest fear was that the curse would be passed on to him and... to us.'

Carys swallowed hard. 'Edward told Father that he had hidden the casket in the darkest of places; difficult to find, and treacherous, too. "Can I trust you? Will you return it? Tell no one of this. His people may know the casket was stolen, that it wasn't destroyed in the fire, or thrown into the Thames." Father repeated his promise; he would keep his secret. Then Edward, this poor man, revealed the hiding place, and passed away just before dawn.'

There was silence in the chapel. The trio thought over this story: the rebellion, the theft of the casket, the plague, and those who had drowned looking for the secret hiding place.

Perils lay ahead. What dangers would they have to face?

There was a long silence. Tara held her bag to her heart and felt the Bronze Mirror.

Simone squeezed her eyes shut and was murmuring, *'O Dio! O Dio mio!'*

'So where is this hiding place?' asked David. 'And if − when − we find the casket, what shall we do with it? Can we keep it? Should we return it to Lord John?' His words were tumbling out. 'Where...?'

Carys frowned. 'We don't know the exact place.'

'Your father − he must have told you,' said Simone.

'He was afraid to. Wat Tyler had been killed by the Mayor of London himself. Stabbed, he was. Even though the rebels hadn't wanted to harm King Richard, they were betrayed by him. Some of the leaders were executed; some, like John Ball, were hung, drawn and quartered. The Peasants' Revolt, they called it. But these people were not peasants; they were jurors, constables, clergy. They owned property.'

'Equality. Justice. That's what they were

fighting for,' said Hugh angrily. 'And they were crushed.'

Carys sighed deeply. 'For years afterwards, Father travelled the Marches, laying his beautiful tiles in the churches, the palaces and castles all around. About the casket, he kept silent.'

'A terrible burden to him, it was,' Hugh said. 'The day before his death, he told us Edward's story, and that he had created a code in case he failed to find the casket. In case he did not return.'

Carys looked at her friends. 'Father said, "Look at my tiles. Follow the clues. It's too dangerous to say more. If James and I are not back in two days, take these tiles here to the castle. The steward is expecting them. But he knows nothing of this secret. Go up to Queen Philippa's chamber. There are tiles in front of the fireplace. Find the pattern, that's the start of a spiral. I've left a clue. It will show you how to find the second part. Go to that place. Look for the next part of the spiral. That will lead you to the third, and last. This have I done in case I do not return. Tell no one..."'

'This is colossal!' said David. 'So we crack the code, find the casket, return it to Lord John, and then he'll give you your lands back.'

'That sounds simple,' muttered Simone.

'Of course it isn't,' said Tara, feeling irritated with her cousin. 'We have to follow the clues, which may not be straightforward. Then we have to find the place where the casket is hidden. And we could all end up being accused of stealing it. This is not simple.'

Simone glared at her. 'I was making a joke.'

'It is very dangerous,' said Carys.

'So where is this code? We don't even know where to start.' Simone folded her arms. 'Do we have to go back to the castle?'

Tara said quietly, 'Carys and I found the pattern in the Queen's chamber. We memorised the tiles. It's like her father said – it's in the shape of a spiral.'

'Cool!' said her twin, moving his finger round in a circle, then around again; a larger one, and then an even bigger circle, and up. He pointed to the heavens. 'Cosmic!'

'The last tile showed the front of the Priory. So the second part of the spiral is here somewhere,' said Carys.

'*Alora*! Let's search for it now,' said Simone, gazing around up at the blue stained-glass windows. 'The sooner we...'

'Tiles, cuz,' said David. 'Try the floor.'

'I know that.'

'No, you're not a bespoiler,' he laughed.

Carys and Hugh grinned.

'What's a–?'

'Hey! Enough!' said Tara.

'When we find the casket, we could take it to our prince, Owain Glyndwr,' said Hugh. 'It could be sold, and help the fight against King Richard.

Then all their harsh laws here in Wales would go. We are not allowed to be here in the town after dark. Only the English.' He looked at David, 'They crush us, you know.' His friend nodded.

'Hugh,' sighed Carys. 'What you say is true. We have been treated badly, since the Normans invaded our lands, but – you keep listening to those men on market days. They fire you up. They are using you. Remember what Father said. They will persuade young lads to fight for a cause, good or bad, and you will be the one who gets thrown in the dungeon. Or worse – get killed, or executed for treason. And the next week, these same men will be spreading their ideas in the market again, looking for the next innocent fellow.'

Hugh looked unhappy. 'But–'

'If you said or did anything against Lord John, we would lose everything.'

'But he won't find out! He–'

Tara touched the Mirror. A whisper came:

Secrets are revealed
In the light of day.
Tell the truth always,
Or you will pay.

'And, as Edward said, violence doesn't solve anything,' added David. 'Believe me, I know.' Memories of lifetimes on Nebula flashed into his mind. He shivered.

'Father and Mother taught us – never take anything that doesn't belong to us,' said Carys.

'Take nothing that has not been freely given.'

The twins nodded. Hugh sighed, and looked away.

Shouts could be heard from the Priory grounds. The puppy began to whine softly.

David grabbed her collar. 'Shush!'

'Lord John's men! They're scouring the town for us!' said Hugh.

They all lay flat along the pews, until the sounds faded away. Only the scream of a fox disturbed the silence.

Tara stood up. 'Let's start looking for the spiral.'

'What about the curse?' said Simone.

'Do you believe in curses?' asked David. 'Really?'

'*Si!* Yes, I do! The casket was in Lord John's palace; it was destroyed. That man – Edward – he died of the plague. The monks did, too. And their father and brother were drowned.' She held her breath. 'The casket must be cursed! We'll all be cursed!'

Tara felt confused. She touched the Mirror. Was this the reason they had come? To lift a curse? To find a casket? It was one thing searching for a will so Eva and her family could keep their land. It was another to search for a cursed casket. *Do I believe in curses?* she wondered. She touched her bag; came the whisper from the Mirror:

Think not the worst,
There is no curse.
Seek the casket high and low.

Hidden in darkness long ago.

She sighed. *Why is it me that has to keep everyone together?* She touched the Mirror again.

Take the breath in,
Hold. Let the breath out.
Slowly, and again,
Never fear, never doubt.

A mind-message. *Are you alright, Twin?*

Yes. I'm fine. The Mirror says we must search for the casket.

'So, come on,' said David. 'Let's find the second spiral and crack the code.'

Carys began examining the tiles in the nearest aisle.

'And just to say – I don't trust that Tristran. Especially after what I told him,' blurted out David.

Tara stared at her brother. 'What did you tell him? I told you to keep *schtum*.'

He cleared his throat. This was bad. 'He was threatening me with the dungeons, because I had played a trick on him with a–' He looked at his sister. She was glaring at him – 'a kind of knight – mummy – stuffed thing they use to practise jousting. Maybe it broke his nose – there was blood. Quite a lot of it, actually.'

'David!'

'It was an accident! Anyway, he went crazy, and I made up this story about a treasure I'd come to find. I didn't know about the casket at the time, did I?' Bethan nuzzled his knee and looked up at him with her dark brown eyes.

Tara mind-messaged her twin. *No, you weren't to know. But you should've remembered to keep schtum anyway. You know stories float around the Universe, and if you catch one you might say something you shouldn't. Well – you did!*

I had to. If they'd thrown me in the dungeons, I wouldn't be here now.

Shaking her head, Tara turned back to the others. 'We need to find the next part of the spiral, before the light goes.'

'Why didn't your father search for this hidden casket?' asked Simone as she glanced around the church.

'He did. That is exactly what he and James were doing when they – when they drowned,' muttered Hugh.

Tara could sense that they were all feeling tired and irritated. But they had to find the code, and soon. She touched the Mirror.

Came the whisper:

Search for the spiral,
Circling around
Otters, herons:
It must be found.

'Spread out. Let's each take an aisle.'

They began to examine the tiled floors, inch by inch. Simone avoided stepping on the slabs with the names of knights and their ladies. *That would definitely bring me bad luck*, she thought.

'How many tiles are there in the spiral?' asked David.

'Seven in each section,' said Carys. She was kneeling on the floor in front of the high altar. 'All these are patterned,' she murmured. 'A flower. Leaves. I can't see–'

Hugh cried out from the Lady Chapel. 'Here's a swan! A white swan. That could be for Mary de Bohun. Henry Bolingbroke's wife.'

Carys looked up. 'In the Queen's chamber, there was a tile with a swan on it. Maybe the second part of the spiral is there. Look carefully, Hugh.'

'Wavy lines – a river!' he called. 'Is this the beginning, do you think?'

Carys went over and stared down at the tile. 'Father and James were on the Wye.'

'There was a coracle in the first spiral. Remember?' said Tara, leaning over her friend's shoulder. 'Perhaps the casket is hidden near a river.'

'Here's an eagle,' said Hugh. 'I saw some high up on the cliffs near Tintern.'

'*O Dio mio!* I won't climb a cliff!' Simone said. 'I'm scared of heights. And stop rolling your eyes, David. You can climb them if you want to.'

'The casket could be high up, in a hollowed-out place, overlooking the river,' said Carys.

'But a sick man couldn't have climbed up there,' said Tara. 'We drove, er – travelled – along there a few days ago, and the cliffs are very steep.'

'Here's a lamprey,' said Hugh.

'What's a lamprey?' asked Simone.

'Fish. Tastes great in a red sauce,' laughed David. 'What?' He glanced at his twin. 'They were cooking it for the feast, and I just had to taste it! It's the abbot's favourite!'

Tara gave him The Look.

'I was hungry! Anyway, come over here and look at this. Long legs, like a statue – it must be–'

'–a heron,' said his twin. 'Water again.'

'And there's another fish – looks like a salmon,' said Hugh.

'What did you say before about a cor–?' asked David.

'A coracle; a small boat.'

'Father and James were in a big boat. We thought they'd been fishing.' Hugh frowned. 'I wish we'd found them both.'

Simone had wandered over to a side chapel, on the right of the high altar. She had lit a candle, and was gazing at the floor.

'Here are some tiles in a strange pattern,' she said. 'It looks different... wavy lines, eagle, lamprey, heron, salmon... an owl... They are curling around in a sort of circle... Does anyone want to look?'

Tara clapped her hands. 'I think she's found it!'

They all rushed over, and peered down at the tiles.

'There are barn owls near–' began Hugh.

'And look at the last one – arches!' cried Carys. 'Tintern Abbey! That's it!' She threw her arms around Simone. 'You've found it! You've found the spiral! *Diolch!* Thank you! Now we can find the casket!'

A branch cracked outside. But none of them heard it. The next part of the puzzle had been solved!

Tara touched the Mirror. Came the whisper:

Leave here now with no fear.
Spin and circle down the river,
To the Abbey
Near the weir.

'How do we get to Tintern Abbey? Is there a boat we can go in?' asked Tara.

'I'll stay here,' said Simone, 'and look after the horse and cart.'

'I told you. I left him with the innkeeper,' said Hugh. 'He'll be fine there.'

'We can all go together. That's the plan, isn't it?' Carys asked Tara.

'What plan? You are always discussing everything with the others.' Simone sat down in a pew and turned away from them.

'You just said you didn't want to come!' David muttered,

Tara glared at him, and hugged her cousin. 'No, we are not leaving you out of this. Who found the document? You did. Who helped Carys feel brave enough to give it to Lady Katherine? You did. You were brilliant! Now, who found the spiral here? You did. We can't do this without you, Simone. Each one of us is needed to complete this task. We're a team. And you are an important part of it.'

Her cousin wiped her eyes. 'Ok. But don't ask me to climb a cliff.'

'We'll send David up if we have to!' laughed Tara. She touched the Mirror again. *Help me, I beg you. It is so hard keeping everyone together. I'm really feeling the pressure here. I – we – need your protection...*

She looked up at the darkening stained-glass windows. 'The light is fading. We have to leave now, and go down the river to Tintern Abbey.'

'There are always some coracles on the bank down by Chippenham Gate,' said Carys. 'I'll steer one. Hugh, you take David and Bethan in yours. Tara and Simone, will you come with me?'

'There won't be enough room in one coracle for you three,' said Hugh.

'Could we tie two together?' asked Tara.

Hugh looked unsure.

'We could go back to your home,' suggested Simone. 'The same way we came.'

'No. We must all go down the river together,' said Tara. 'We can all squeeze into two coracles.'

Her cousin twisted her hair around her finger. 'But–'

'We must leave this minute, cuz.'

'Keep to the shadows,' whispered Carys, as they crept out of the Priory and made their way towards the riverbank.

Behind them a figure followed, then hid itself amongst the willows.

Chapter 11
On the River

The sun was at its lowest in the sky: streaks of red and purple were scratched just above the line of hills. The midsummer moon was rising as they arrived at the riverbank.

'We'll borrow these,' said Hugh, pointing to two coracles that were upside-down on the grass. 'They belong to our neighbours.'

He turned the frail boats over.

Simone stared at them. 'Couldn't we borrow a bigger one? Then we could all fit in one.'

'There isn't a bigger one here,' said Hugh.

'We can squash in,' said Carys. 'It'll be fine.'

'But it looks too cramped for–' began David. Then he felt The Look from his twin.

'Be very careful how you get in,' said Hugh, as he picked up the paddle, 'or you'll fall in the river. Sit on the strut in the middle.'

David was holding the puppy tightly. She squirmed. 'Stay still. I'm going to step in and keep us both balanced. Oh, it's swaying!'

The coracle rocked from side to side. 'Argh!'

'Quick! Sit down,' said Hugh.

Bethan jumped out of David's arms and sat in the back, whimpering.

'Are you OK?' called Tara.

'Now, I am. Wobbled a bit. Mind how you get in.'

'See you at the Abbey.'

Hugh pushed off from the bank, turned the coracle with ease in a figure of eight, and moved with the swirling currents.

'Keep the paddle shallow in the water,' called his sister. 'The river is very high from the storms the other night.'

As he tried to steer the flimsy boat, it began to spin, like a feather in the wind. 'This is the highest I've ever seen the river. And fast-flowing, too.'

Tara stood on the bank, and watched as the boys and the puppy disappeared around the bend. *Keep them safe, O Goddess*, she begged.

Carys was trying to coax Simone into the other coracle.

'*Alora!* There are too many of us for this tiny boat,' said the girl. 'I'll stay here. It'll be better. I'm going to fall in. We'll cap– cap–'

'Capsize,' said Tara, as she stepped in and sat on the strut. 'Come on in, Simone.'

'Oh, it's rocking.'

'Just get in. Carys will be in the middle, with the paddle. There's enough room.'

'*O Dio mio*,' muttered Simone, as she took one

step into the coracle. She quickly sat down, and clung on to the side of the little boat. *Another nightmare*, she thought. *I'm going to be sick, it's wobbling so much.*

'There, we're in, and we'll all meet at the landing place, just by the Abbey,' said Carys. Pushing off from the bank, she turned and twisted the coracle into and out of the currents. 'Swirling and swinging, we are,' she said.

May we all arrive safely, thought Tara, as she admired the skill of her friend.

A few minutes later, a third coracle entered the river. Immediately, it struggled against the currents, was tossed this way and that; then, caught in a whirlpool, around and around it spun. Someone was not used to steering such a boat, and not on a river in full flood.

The Wye carried the boys' coracle under the bridge at Bigsweir, and towards the Abbey. Stars were coming out, clustering together: the moon seemed vast and glowing in the night sky.

'So, tell. What happened at the market?' David held Bethan tightly, and kept checking to see how far they were from the riverbank.

He noticed a kingfisher, perched on a snag of a

twig, looking for minnows and sticklebacks. Further down, a brown shape slipped into the waters, curled around, and vanished into the gloom.

Was that an otter? he wondered. *If we end up in the water, can I swim that far? These currents are very strong. This feels like being on a rollercoaster.*

'I heard a lot of gossip,' answered Hugh. 'Thomas, Lord of Gloucester, has been trying to get his Welsh tenants to fight with him for the king, but they refused!' He laughed as he used the paddle to switch this way and that. 'And Gwenneth Davies, who has a stall selling clothes, got into a row with Rhys Williams, the blacksmith.'

'Why was that?' David was trying to focus on staying still as the boat pitched and rolled. *Oh, I feel sick.* He clutched his stomach. *Maybe it was the beavers' tails. I can't tell Mum and Dad about that.*

'With so many men dying of the plague, the women have to sell things now. And some men are just angry about that. I don't understand why.' He switched hands, and swivelled the boat sideways. 'Gwenneth is very funny. "I heard your wife divorced you for bad breath, Rhys Williams," she said. And everyone laughed at him. He went red. He was very angry!'

'Can you do that?'

'By the laws of Wales, you can!'

'That's brilliant!'

'So – the market?' David had closed his eyes, and was stroking the spaniel's head. *This will end*, he thought. *Please let this end soon.*

They glided on for some minutes in silence.

'Don't tell Carys.'

'You can trust me.'

'She'll be very angry with me.'

'Believe me, I know all about older sisters being cross.'

Hugh paused, as a barn owl glided past and hooted. 'I was playing some of my tunes, people were enjoying them, humming along, some were throwing coins. Then, after a while, I felt hungry. So I bought an eel pasty. I love eel pasties.'

David smiled. 'So does Bethan! What happened then?'

'Someone shouted that their purse had been stolen. I saw a young boy running off towards the bridge, but the baker pointed at me. I don't know why. He knows me. "These coins are not real! They're fake! It must be him! Hugh ap Morgan! There he is! Catch him!" "He's a thief! Hang him!" People were shouting, "Put him in the stocks!" Bethan started barking at them all. A man tried to grab her. It was terrible. A trader was shouting, "In my country, you would be boiled alive for forging money!"'

'Boiled alive? Hang you?' David was shocked. 'How come?' He clutched the puppy tightly; she shifted herself and nestled under his arm.

'Over seven years old, you can be hung for stealing anything. The blacksmith was just about to put me upside-down in the stocks when Vincenzo – remember the trader from Italy, who gave us the pouches? Well, he told them he'd seen the thief running off towards Monnow Bridge. So then a few men chased after him down the street.'

'What about the coins?'

'Vincenzo paid the baker for my pasty. There have been lots of these counterfeit coins around here, he said. No one knows who's been doing it.'

'Can I see them when we land?'

'Here, have them. I don't want them. They've only brought me trouble.'

'Thanks.' David put the coins in his pouch. 'Did you stay in the market?'

'No, I picked up Bethan, and ran to the cart. We hid under the cloth, and didn't move. I won't be going back to Monmouth market for months. Maybe I'll go to Chepstow instead.'

'Hey, puppy. You've had a rough time,' said David as he stroked her floppy ears.

'She's a good dog. Defended me against those bullies, she did. Maybe…'

'She can't stay, Hugh. Sorry. She's coming home with me… eventually…' David stared into the black waters swirling around them. *When might that be?* he wondered.

Hugh glanced down at the puppy. He was feeling guilty that she'd almost got beaten by the blacksmith. It was at this point that he dipped the paddle in too deeply.

'Hugh! What are you doing?'

Spinning wildly around, the little craft crashed into rocks in the middle of the river. The spaniel yelped as she was flung out into the darkness.

'Bethan! Where are you? I can't see you! Bethan!' shouted David, frantically trying to catch sight of her. The coracle lurched and swayed.

'If she drowns—'

'I'm sorry. I forgot there were rocks around here,' wailed Hugh, as he turned the boat around and around, searching for the puppy. The light had gone; it was now pitch-black.

'Bethan! Where are you?' called David. 'Bethan!' There was silence. 'How could you?' he shouted at Hugh. 'You—'

'Dogs always find their way back home. She'll be alright.'

'Home?' David was furious. 'She doesn't know where home is. I don't know where home is. My parents gave her to us when we left London. She's a rescue dog, and the most beautiful, adorable and loving puppy—'

David wiped away the tears that were now streaming down his cheeks. He shouted at Hugh again. 'She could be lost and wandering around in the forest; attacked, ripped apart by a wild boar. We must get out and look for her now.'

He glared up at Hugh.

'But we have to meet Carys at the Abbey, and find the next part of the spiral. We have to find the casket...'

'I don't care about any old gold, silver or treasure. Bethan is much more important, much more valuable, than old tiles and a – a casket. She's a living, breathing being.' David wiped his wet face, and stared into the night. 'Bethan!' he shouted. 'Bethan!'

Hugh steered as fast as he could towards the riverbank. *I was scared of Simone*, he thought. *Now, terrified of David I am. He's so angry with me. Maybe he'll punch me. We have to find his dog.*

With a sweep of the paddle, Carys brought the coracle onto the shore by the Abbey. She looked around. 'That's strange. The boys left before us.'

Tara jumped out. 'Oh – squelchy! It's muddy, Simone. Watch where you put your feet.'

She stepped carefully through the oozing, muddy slime. *I wish I was wearing boots, or wellies*, she thought, as she lifted one foot and then the other. 'Yuk!' The slippery brown liquid clung to her woollen hose. 'Nasty!'

'We can leave the boat here,' said Carys. 'It won't be high tide for another ten or eleven hours.'

They dragged the coracle up the bank, turned it over, and left it under some willow trees.

'Where are the boys and Bethan?' asked Simone as she picked bits of twig off her tunic.

None of them heard another craft being beached further up the river.

The three leaned back against their small boat, and looked in the direction of the Abbey. Lights were flickering in the nearest building.

'That's their guest house,' said Carys. 'Father sometimes stayed there in the winter when he was working here.'

'*O Dio mio!* What's that?'

Sounds of crashing, followed by shouting and calling, came from the woods. Then silence.

'Outlaws or poachers,' whispered Carys. 'Don't move.'

Minutes later, they heard rustling in the undergrowth.

Simone jumped. 'Ah–!'

'That'll be a boar, or maybe a fox looking for its dinner.'

'Don't worry, cuz,' said Tara. 'We're too big!'

'Oh, I'm so hungry. Let's knock on the door of the Abbey, and ask the monks for something to eat.'

'Only men and boys are allowed in there,' said Carys. 'We'll have to stay here while they go inside and search for the last part of the spiral.'

'Could they bring some food out to us?'

'Maybe they've gone in already, and are sleeping

in the dormitory. Warm and cosy,' said Tara.

'While we are sitting here, starving and shivering, with our ankles and toes covered in...!' said Simone.

'...mud and slime,' said her cousin.

The moon appeared from behind a cloud, as a coracle came around the bend. Two bedraggled-looking boys with a filthy puppy jumped out onto the bank. Bethan bounded up to Simone, shook herself, and tried to lick the girl's face.

'Ergh! Get off me, Bethan! *Disgusto!* You smell horrible, and you've shaken more mud all over me!'

The spaniel wagged her tail, barked, then lay on her back, with her legs waving in the air.

'Sit!' Tara commanded. The dog stared up at her, jumped up, then sat. 'Good girl!'

Tara turned to see the boys pulling their little boat up on the grass. Water was dripping from their clothes.

'What–?'

'We hit some rocks, and Bethan – er – she fell out,' said Hugh.

'You hit some rocks. And then you told me she would find her way home – Home! How stup–'

Twin! Tara mind-messaged her brother. She could see the young boy was feeling guilty. *Calling him names is not good. Remember, he's too used to being bullied. Try to be kind...*

David took a few deep breaths and nodded. 'So Hugh steered us onto the bank, and we searched for Bethan. I'm surprised you didn't hear us calling for her.'

'We thought you were thieves – or poachers–'

'So we kept zippy – er – zipped.'

'After searching for hours – well, a few minutes, she found us. Bounding towards us and wagging her tail–'

'She thought it was a game,' added Hugh.

David glared at him. 'So we got back in the coracle, and here we are. No thanks–'

'Shush!' hissed Tara. 'We're all here, and we're safe.'

David groaned. 'I think those beaver tails have given me stomach cramps.'

'Or it could be that fish – the lamprey – in a rich red sauce,' added Simone.

He frowned. 'You're loving this, aren't you, cuz?'

She grinned.

'Stop it, you two!' Tara was growing impatient with all of them. 'Peace!' She turned to Hugh. 'You know the Abbey. Have you got an idea where the third part of the spiral could be?'

David said crossly, 'Oh, just ask the Mirror.'

'I will not,' she replied firmly. 'We have to go through this task on our own. We must think for ourselves. When things get difficult, we just have to try our best to sort it out. You of all people, Twin, know that we are on this planet to learn. And we need to stick together.'

'Be a team,' said David hurriedly, knowing how

definite his sister could be at these times. Some might call it bossy, he grinned, then caught Tara's eye.

Remember, she mind-messaged him, *No anger, or we won't complete this task...*

'Truce?' said David, turning to Hugh and Simone.

'Truce.'

They all sat down on the riverbank. The clear night air carried all the sounds: snapping of twigs, snuffling of hedgehogs, snorting of wild boar. The moon had risen higher, and the sky was filled with millions of stars.

Simone wriggled: the ground was damp. *I'd better not mention it*, she thought. *Everyone is cross.* Bethan came over and nuzzled her. 'Good girl,' she whispered as she stroked her. 'You've had an adventure, haven't you? I think you want to be at home, too. Maybe it won't be long now.'

The puppy put her head in her lap and dozed off.

'What about this for a plan? You boys ring the bell at the gate, and ask the monk if you can stay the night,' said Tara.

'The guest house is over there.' Hugh waved his hand towards the Abbey.

'So, when the monks are asleep, we'll sneak out of our room and search around for the last part of the spiral,' said David, adding, 'Hugh told me the monastery is vast... lots of chapels, the abbot's apartments, cloisters...'

'… a chapter house…'

'Right, that too. Anyway, we'll find the spiral, memorise the order of the tiles, then creep back into the guest house, until the monks get up for the next service. Matins, did you say?'

The young boy nodded. 'Two o'clock.'

'Then we'll slip out and come back here.'

'And we can discuss what to do next,' said Tara. 'Is that alright with everyone?'

They nodded.

'Promise not to say anything about the casket to the monks, Twin.'

'Yes, but why?' asked David.

'If the treasure is found on their land, they will claim it. And they are very wealthy,' said Carys.

'The casket belongs to Lord John,' said her brother.

'That's why we must keep quiet about it until we find it,' said Tara. 'Agreed?'

'Agreed.'

'And there is something else,' said Tara.

'What?'

'I don't know.' She took a deep breath. 'One step at a time.'

'At least Tristran isn't around. He wanted the treasure to buy armour and a horse,' said David. 'So he could be a knight.'

Tara touched the Mirror.

People want,
People strive,

Those who want,
Will never thrive.

'We'll need a story to tell the monks, though,' said Hugh.

'Keep close to the truth, but tell no lies,' said Tara.

'What about this: We came down the river. It was high tide, and very dangerous after the storms of the other night. We hit rocks and fell out, so we're very wet,' suggested her twin.

'And we landed here. So may we have shelter for the night?' added Hugh.

'*Bene*. That sounds good,' said Simone, yawning.

Noticing an arch of willows nearby, Tara pointed to it. 'If we huddle together under those trees, we should be warm enough. Come on, Bethan. You're a girl. You can't go into the Abbey, either! See you later, boys.'

'Carys laughed, 'Let's snuggle up together; *cwtch* up!'

Leaving the landing area, the boys followed the path towards the Abbey.

'Do you know where we're going?' asked David.

'There are two gateways here. I think we need to go to the second one.'

'You think.'

'I only came here twice with Father. The barns and stables are over there.'

The two boys felt their way along the high walls surrounding the monastery. A chill wind whipped around them.

'Here's the bell.'

'Well, ring it.' David was cold, tired, and getting impatient.

A shadow, a shape, crept behind a gnarled old oak tree, to watch, to wait, to listen.

Chapter 12
In the Abbey

Hugh and David stood in front of the gateway.

'What do we do now?' asked David as he jumped up and down, flapping his arms. 'I'm so wet and cold! Ring the bell again.'

Hugh pulled the rope hanging by the entrance. 'The porter will come and let us in. They have to. It's the rule.'

David gazed up at the clouds racing across the moon. 'Awesome!' he exclaimed. 'You'd never see a sky like this in London.'

The wind whistled around the walls. Footsteps hurried across the courtyard.

'*Quo vadis?*'

'What did he say?' asked David.

'He's asked who we are... or where are we going... Something like that... It's Latin.'

'Don't they speak English here?'

'Yes! French and Welsh, too!'

'*Bore da!* It's Hugh, son of Owen ap Morgan, from Trellech, Brother. And I've a friend with me, David er – ap Jones.'

The oak door creaked open. A short, sturdy man in a black and white robe stood there, rubbing his eyes.

'Come in! Come in! Welcome! *Croeso!*'

'*Diolch!* Thank you, Brother.'

'Follow me to the guest house. I'll take you to the rooms for important visitors. It's empty at the moment.'

'We're important,' grinned David.

'You are. You are. Every being is important. Come along, boys. Sit here in the guest hall, and I'll bring you both some pottage. You can sleep in the dormitory.'

'You're very kind,' said David. 'We are so cold, wet–'

'–and very hungry,' added Hugh.

'Ah, look at you! Waifs and strays! What have you been doing?'

The bedraggled lads stood shivering in the middle of the hall; their faces were smeared in slime, and muddied paw prints were all over their tunics.

'We came from Monmouth in a coracle, and had an accident by Bigsweir–'

'Ah – yes, those rocks...' The monk shook his head. 'Now, sit closer to the fire; there's still some warmth left in it, I see. I'll bring you water to wash your face and hands. We have some spare tunics. I'll look for them while you're eating.'

'*Diolch.* Thank you, Brother.'

'We're very sorry we woke you up,' added David.

'It will be Matins soon. So only a few minutes more sleep. That's all I would have had,' smiled the monk.

'Oh, this mattress is comfortable,' said Hugh, as they lay in the dormitory, listening to the monks making their way down the stairs to the main church.

'I'm so tired. We could have a good night's sleep, and search for the spiral in the morning.'

'No, we can't,' said David. 'Imagine facing Tara. You don't even want to think of that, my friend. We have to go back with the goods.'

'The goods?'

'The code – the list of tiles.' He yawned.

'So, what's the time of their next service?'

'Lauds. Five o'clock. Father taught us about their day. They sleep little.'

'That means we haven't got much time to find the spiral.'

Hugh turned over. 'I suppose you're right.'

'We'll wait until after this service. The monks will go back to sleep, then we'll creep into the church and... Oh, so sleepy...'

Hugh didn't answer. *The third part of the spiral*

could be anywhere in the Abbey, he thought. *But I shan't tell David that. He might get angry with me again.*

Aloud, he said, 'I wonder how the others are.'

'Not as comfortable as we are,' laughed David, as he closed his eyes.

The three girls lay under the willows, listening to the wind gusting around them. Bethan had squeezed in between Tara and Simone, and was making dream noises.

'I don't expect we'll get much sleep tonight,' said Carys. 'But we'll be safe here until the boys come back–'

'The ground is so cold and wet. We'll end up with new – p-neu – something nasty,' said Simone as she wriggled closer to the puppy. 'I don't know why I'm hugging Bethan. She's covered in mud!'

Tara sighed. It was difficult enough trying to work out the next step of the quest without her cousin complaining all the time. Perhaps this was her mission, to help Simone to be more positive in life. She sighed again. *Sometimes I feel I'm like a mother! I'm twelve!* She touched the Mirror. But there were no whispers. No answers. Silence. Only the wind.

'Tell us a story, Carys,' said Simone. 'It'll help to pass the time.'

'What about?'

'Anything.'

'A few years ago,' the young Welsh girl began, 'people saw strange lights in the sky. This went on for seven nights. All over the country, you could see them. No one knew what they were, but some said that they were omens.'

'Omens?' asked Simone.

'Signs, that something terrible was going to happen. More plagues, wars, disasters...'

'Did everyone believe this?' asked Tara.

'Some, not everyone,' she said. 'But then taxes increased, and people rebelled against the king; our prince here in Wales began to gather men to fight for our freedom.' She paused. 'I believe in freedom and justice for everyone, but I feel bloodshed will surely come to our land...'

They stared up at the stars scattered over the dark night sky.

'Such beauty with wonders beyond,' whispered Tara.

'Omens. Signs,' said Simone. 'It could be aliens.'

'Aliens?' asked Carys. 'What are they?'

Before Tara could stop her, her cousin was talking about Martians, and beings from other planets that change their shape. 'They probably built the pyramids of Egypt!' she ended triumphantly.

Carys smiled. 'Truly, Simone, you are a great *seanacht*. A teller of marvellous tales.'

'I'm thinking of becoming an actor. Ouch! What are you doing, Tara?' Simone exclaimed as her cousin prodded her gently in the back.

Bethan jumped in her sleep, looked around, and quickly settled back down, snuggling between her friends.

'Who knows what worlds exist out there...' murmured Carys.

A red lamp was glowing in the Abbey church as Hugh and David slipped in through a side entrance. All was silent. The monks had returned to their cells. Two candles only had been left alight on the high altar.

'Do you think your father laid the tiles in the main part of the church?'

Hugh began scanning the floor in front of him. 'I'm not sure. He worked on the abbot's new apartments. But only a few monks are allowed in there. Father would not have made the spiral so difficult to find.'

David glanced around. There were side chapels to the left and to the right. A red lamp was burning in each one. 'It will take us ages to examine each section of the floor carefully.'

A mind-message came from Tara: *You must be away before dawn. Sunrise will come early...*

'Let's take a candle each,' David suggested. 'Then we can search up and down the aisles. It'll be quicker. You take the left, and I'll take the right.'

Hugh knelt down, blessed himself, and prayed, 'Please help us.' Then he took the two candles from the altar, gave one to his friend, and went over to the left aisle. After several minutes, they met by the choir stalls.

'Patterns – flowers and diamonds. Nothing that looks like a spiral.'

'No,' sighed David. 'Maybe it's in the abbot's quarters after all, or somewhere else. We are stuffed.'

'Stuffed?'

'I mean, there aren't any clues here.' He shook his head. 'Oh, if only Tara were here, she could ask the Mirror.'

'Where did you find it?' asked Hugh. 'How does it work?'

There was a slight movement at the back of the church. A figure slid quietly in and hid behind a stone pillar.

'It was buried in the ground, not far from here, on top of a hill. Near your home, actually. She touches it. It tells her things. And that's how we came here. I think it's thousands of years old. I'm not exactly sure. It's something to do with–' David felt a painful twinge on his earlobe. 'Argh! Oh!'

'What's the matter?'

'A stabbing pain. It's nothing.' *Just a sharp reminder to keep schtum*, he thought. *Will I ever learn? No wonder the Mirror was given to my sister. She's opaque.* He smiled. The Sphinx, they called her on Craxia 3.

'Do you know where the abbot's apartments are?'

Hugh swung around to answer, 'Father wouldn't have—' His candle toppled and fell to the floor. Wax immediately spread out over the tiles.

'Oh no! We'll have to get it off before it goes hard – quickly!'

Placing his candlestick on the floor, David knelt down and began wiping the wax up with his sleeve. He stopped.

'Hugh! Look! This is it!' Scraping furiously at the wax, he exclaimed, 'Brilliant! Here's an otter! Of course! The third spiral had to be bigger than the one in the Priory.'

He kept scraping. 'Look, Hugh, here's the pattern. Round and round and up! Come on. Help me!'

The boy threw himself on the floor, and began wiping the wax up. 'A water vole... a lamprey. Why are there two lampreys in the spiral?'

'Maybe your father wanted to make sure we really noticed them. It could be a major clue.' David traced over the next tile. 'Something hanging upside-down?'

'A bat!'

'I can't make this one out. Wavy lines, but–'

'A river. Father always did that for water.'

'There's a shape above it. Curved. Dark. What do you think that is, Hugh?' David sat back on his ankles. 'Could it be a cave?'

Hugh grinned. 'Got it! It's the cave. It must be! That's why Father put two lampreys in the spiral.'

'What cave?'

'The Lamprey Cave. No one ever goes in it!'

'Why?'

'It's very dangerous. Anyone who has gone in has never come out.'

'Edward did.'

The two boys thought about the man who had kept his secret for so long, and had died near where they were kneeling.

Hugh stared at the pattern. 'Here's a tile with things hanging down like long, thin drips of water. Others – stretching; reaching upwards. Strange shapes. What are they?'

'These could be stalactites and stalagmites, found in caverns deep down below the surface of the Earth...'

Hugh shivered. 'Do we dare to go in this cave?'

'To find the casket? asked his friend. 'That's what we have come for. We are brave enough, aren't we?' He examined the tiles again. 'Here it is. You're right! A blue and golden image – a peacock carved on the lid of a box.'

'The casket!'

A slight sound came from behind the curtain.

'What's that?'

'Probably a mouse,' said Hugh.

'We haven't any paper – I mean parchment. Let's remember the order these tiles are in. There are seven. We'll remember them better if we touch them at the same time.'

As the boys ran their fingers over the tiles, they repeated the letters several times: 'O, V, L, B, C, S, C.'

A door banged.

'Who are you?' came a shout from the back of the church. 'What are you doing? Chanting! Witchcraft!'

'Father Abbot!' cried Hugh.

David recognised the man from the feast. His face was contorted, eyes flashing as he stormed down the aisle. 'In God's house, we'll have none of this blasphemy!'

'No! No! We are – we were only admiring my father's workmanship.'

'And praying for his soul,' said David.

'And for my brother James,' added Hugh. 'We were saying a – a litany.'

Father Abbot put his arms inside the sleeves of his robe and glowered at the two boys.

David put his arm around his friend's shoulder. 'He's been in such grief since his father and brother were drowned at the weir that he felt he had to come here; to see and touch the last thing that – that his dear father had made.' He crossed his fingers behind his back. 'It was such a terrible shock.' Then, remembering the conversation he'd overheard at the feast, he shook his head sadly. 'As you know, Father Abbot, the level of the water by the weir had changed, and... well, people are saying that's why the accident happened...'

'You are blaming me for their deaths?' The abbot became even angrier. 'How dare you accuse me!' He raised his hand as he moved threateningly towards the boys.

David softened his voice. 'It's not good to be eaten up inside with guilt – or anger.' He sighed and shook his head. 'It only hurts you, your inner self, in the end.' He paused. 'It's very bad for your health, as well you know. High blood pressure. You could have a heart attack, or a stroke, and be paralysed.'

'Get OUT!' screamed the abbot, waving his arms around.

David dodged the monk. 'Your teeth are so rotten. You really should eat less sugar!' he called as they hurtled down the aisle and out of the church.

'Now where are we?'

Hugh grabbed David's arm. 'Not sure. Let's try this way.'

They raced along a row of arches.

'This is the Cloisters,' said Hugh. 'If he finds us, he'll lock us in the cellars.'

A nearby door opened. Diving into the shadows,

they saw a monk, his eyes cast down, walking silently towards the church.

'He's come out of the Book Room,' whispered Hugh. 'We can hide in there until all the monks are back in church. They'll be singing away, and the abbot won't be able to search for us. But how can we escape? Everything is locked up.'

'We'll just have to climb over the walls.'

The pale light of dawn began to soften the darkness. Simone stirred, and started flapping at her face. '*No!* Get off! Stop licking me!' Bethan lay back down again.

'Are you awake, Tara? I'm so cold. I didn't sleep. When are we going home? Are the boys back yet?'

'Not yet. Shush a minute. Listen! Is that a blackbird? Or a thrush?' said Tara.

Her cousin groaned. 'I'm just not a morning person.'

I hadn't noticed. Tara grinned. 'Just breathe slowly,' she said. 'And keep believing.'

'*Sí.* Keep believing,' murmured her cousin. 'And I am breathing!' She sat up and glanced around. 'Oh, Carys is over there, by the riverbank.'

The young girl was watching the mist rise; wisps curling, floating up the sides of the steep valley. Trees were thickening with leaves of light green and bronze gold. Clouds brushed across the sky.

Simone strolled over and sat next to her. 'It's very beautiful here.'

Carys smiled. 'Listen. Can you hear the lark? And there's the woodpecker – now a jay.' She sighed deeply. 'Hugh makes up lovely songs with their melodies.

Tara stood looking at the Wye, and the reflections of the oaks and birches. 'It's stunning here. And it still is, in our time. But all over our world, millions of trees have been cut down. So many animals and birds have nowhere to live. They are getting fewer and fewer. Imagine a world without birdsong?'

Carys looked horrified. 'No! That can't be! There would only be – silence. Spring would be silent.'

'There are people working hard to change this though, aren't they, cuz?' said Simone as she picked some daisies and began to make a chain.

'Yes, especially young people. They don't want to grow up on a planet where the rivers are filthy and the air they breathe chokes them.'

'Truly, you come from a different world,' said Carys sadly.

'And that's why we came to this valley: to help protect the woods, the birds, hedgehogs, badgers… and keep the river clean.'

'I think I'll make a flower necklace–'

Loud crashing sounds came from the bushes behind them. The puppy leapt up, sniffed the air, and raced towards the noise. A pheasant broke cover and scurried across the path.

'No, Bethan! Stop!'

'It could be a poacher,' whispered Simone.

'Or outlaws...'

'Bore da!' The boys grinned. Bits of bramble were stuck in their hair, and strands of ivy clung to their tunics.

'I shan't be visiting the Abbey again for a while,' said Hugh as he bent over, trying to catch his breath. 'The abbot was furious with us. He thought we were doing witchcraft. And when David told him getting angry was bad for his health, he went even redder in the face. It was so funny!'

'I was just trying to be helpful.'

'Maybe telling him to stop eating sugar did it!'

Carys looked serious. 'We could get into terrible trouble with the Church, Hugh.'

'No, we said we were praying, like a litany. I think he believed that bit–'

'Then we hid in the Book Room, and while all the monks were in church singing and praying...'

'... we raced around the whole Abbey, looking for a way to escape.'

'I gave him a leg up over a wall by the kitchens. And then–'

'Right–' smiled Tara, seeing the boys were friends again, but knowing this story could go on for a while. 'So – what did you find out?'

'Did you discover the last part of the spiral?'

asked Simone. 'That was what you were going for, after all.'

David frowned. 'Yes, we did, actually. We had to crawl all over the church, and the side chapels, too – on our knees, staring at each tile. And then the candle fell, and–'

'David!' said Tara.

'Alright! You tell it, Hugh.'

The young boy grinned. 'We found the spiral. It was in St Katherine's chapel. Then we memorised the letters in the right order.'

'I don't understand. What letters?' asked Simone.

'The first letter of each word. It makes it easier to learn, cuz.'

'I know that!'

'So,' said David, 'O is for–'

'Otter, then V for vole – water vole, L – lamprey,' recited Hugh.

'Lamprey again?'

'Yes – we think Father did that deliberately, and–'

'B – for bat,' said David.

'C for cave with a river entrance.'

'S – for – get this – stalactites and stalagmites! Awesome!'

'And,' Hugh paused, 'C for casket!'

'If we work out the clues, we can find the casket!'

'Bats!' said Simone. 'I hate bats! You can catch diseases from them, and they live in caves. Yuk!'

'But what does this mean?' asked Tara.

'All these live on or near the river,' said Carys. 'We've already come this far down the Wye. Father and James didn't get further than Bigsweir, so it must be further on.'

'There are otters, water voles and lamprey between here and Chepstow,' said Hugh.

'A cave? So the casket must be hidden in the Lamprey Cave,' murmured Carys. 'We'll have to go in the coracles again down to–'

'*O Dio mio!* No!' said Simone. 'That journey was terrifying. It was so dark; we were all squashed up. I thought we were going to drown.'

'Well, we survived,' said Tara firmly. 'And we are going to see this task through and complete it.' *The first of the quest*, she thought as she touched the Mirror.

Otter and lamprey,
Now three must be brave
Bats and eagle,
Seek, enter the cave.

She turned to their friends. 'So there's an entrance into the cave from the riverbank?'

'Yes! Lamprey Cave,' said Hugh. 'It's a few miles from here.' He exchanged looks with his sister.

'It must be very dangerous.' Simone looked at them. 'I won't go in.'

There was a long pause.

'We have two choices,' said David. 'Either we try, or we don't.'

'I have been told... Three of us have to go into the

cave and search for the casket,' said Tara.

At the river's edge, a shape slid into the cold, muddy waters; twisted, and dived down, down into the depths.

'We're wasting time,' said David. 'Let's go. Let's do it!'

The boys lifted up their coracle. Bethan jumped up, ran around in a circle, wagged her tail furiously, and barked.

Tara helped Carys with the second coracle. 'We'll go first, and the boys next. Is that agreed?'

'Simone, you sit on my left, and Tara on my right, like before. Then I'll paddle down river towards the cave. It's not far.'

Tara got in and held out her hand. 'Come on, cuz.'

Simone hesitated, stepped in, and gripped the side. 'O... O...'

A heron was standing on a flat rock, studying the fast-flowing river. Swifts swooped and spun in the midsummer air.

'Let's hope the currents by the cave are not too strong. We don't want to be carried way down to Chepstow and out to sea,' muttered Hugh as he picked up the paddle.

David caught hold of Bethan and stepped into the coracle. It wobbled slightly. *Perhaps I can learn to do this when we get home*, he thought. *I might even get good at it.*

'Are you alright, David?' asked Hugh, worried that they may have another disaster.

'Yes. Let's go!'

Carys set off first, then her brother. They steered their small boats in figures of eight, gradually making their way down the river. The sun rose higher in the clear blue sky.

'There's the Devil's Pulpit,' said Hugh, waving at the woods opposite the Abbey.

'Don't take your hands off the paddle!' David shouted, as the coracle spun around. 'Tell me later. Just keep steering in the right direction!'

He held the spaniel tightly to his heart. *Next week, when we're home, we can walk down here. That's if we ever make it back home.* He stroked Bethan's head. 'Good girl. Stay calm. Whatever happens...'

Carys beached the coracle on a bank a few miles down from the Abbey. The cliffs above them were sheer. Tara stepped out of the boat and looked up. Here were those craggy rocks they had driven past yesterday, or was it the day before? Had they lost days as well as weeks? When they got back home, what year would it be? Would they even be in the twenty-first century? Would they ever get back? She shook herself. *Never give up, never doubt.*

David and Hugh arrived at the cave's entrance

just as Simone was announcing again that she wasn't going inside.

'I hate bats. They smell. I hate places that are small. I get claust–'

'Claustrophobic.'

'Yes, that. There may be a curse, and there's a disease you can get.' She wiped her eyes. 'I want to see my parents again. I'm scared.'

Tara hugged her. 'It's OK to be scared, cuz.'

'We're all frightened, Simone,' said Carys.

'Perhaps we should toss a coin to decide who goes in,' said David. He took out the leather pouch, and felt for the coins Hugh had given him from the market.

Carys stepped forward. 'I must go in. It was my father and brother who died trying to find the casket.' She looked at her brother. 'You are small. Maybe the places inside are narrow and so–'

'–I could wriggle through.' Hugh nodded, but he looked terrified.

Tara stared at the entrance. 'The Mirror said three had to go in.'

She mind-messaged David, *Twin, will you stay here with Bethan and wait for us? Can you look after Simone?*

'That's cool. I'll just hang around here and wait for you, he replied. *And make sure Bethan doesn't get lost.* He fussed the spaniel.

Tara turned to face Carys and Hugh. 'It's decided. I'll go into the cave with you.'

'We are going to need some light,' said Carys.

'Here are some candles from the Abbey. I'll leave some money for them next time,' Hugh said hurriedly, glancing at his sister. 'And I've got flint and a tinderbox.'

Simone stared at the three of them. 'No. You can't – I may never see–'

Her cousin shook her head. 'Good thoughts, cuz. Only good thoughts.'

Tara, Carys and Hugh stood in front of the entrance to the cave. It was dark and forbidding.

'There may be skeletons in there... spirits,' whispered the young boy. He lit a candle.

Their journey into the deep darkness had begun.

☆☆☆ Chapter 13
Into the Darkness

Shadows played over the rock walls: bats flitted past, disappearing into the blackness beyond.

'Whatever happens,' said Tara, 'we must trust each other. And not give up.'

The brother and sister nodded.

'Breathe slowly. Stay calm. Now–'

With every step, there was a slurping sound.

'It's difficult to walk in this thick mud,' said Carys.

'And to see in this darkness,' said Tara, peering through the gloom. *Even taking one step forward is hard*, she thought.

Hugh waved the candle around; the light from the flame flickered over the low ceiling.

As they went along, they could see piles of boulders on either side.

'Rock falls,' said Carys.

'Maybe Edward left the casket around here. Keep a look out.'

Suddenly, a sheer wall of rock appeared in front

of them. The entrance had come to an abrupt end.

'The cave – it can't just be this opening,' said Tara. 'It has to go back further than this.'

'Cold air,' said Carys. 'Where's it coming from?'

'Look!' said Hugh. 'Over there! A split in the rock! It's very narrow. Shall I try and crawl through?'

'Yes. Maybe there's a bigger cave beyond,' said his sister. Panic was rising up; she felt the solid rock walls pressing down on her, closing in. Her breath became shallower. 'Tara – my head... my...'

'Take deep breaths,' said Tara. She touched the Mirror. 'Protect and guide us. I beg you...' she murmured.

'Simone was right. It smells terrible.'

'Hold the candle, while I try to get through this gap,' said Hugh.

He put his head and shoulders through first, then began to squeeze his body through the fissure.

'I-I'm stuck.'

'Try and move your shoulders,' called Tara.

'I can't. And the dark – it's...' Hugh squirmed. 'Argh!'

'What?'

'I've grazed my knees... I'm alright...'

Several minutes passed; the girls sat on the rocks, shivering, waiting.

'This is too hard. We should go back,' said Carys.

Just then, her brother called. 'You'll have to twist and turn, but you can get through.'

'You go first. Take the candle. I'll feel my way,' said Tara.

'But–'

'Go on. I'll be fine.'

Crawling between the rocks, Carys forced an arm through the gap.

'Take the candle, Hugh. Oh... It's difficult... Don't come behind me yet, Tara. I don't want to kick you.'

She moved forward once more, sliding her body through the crack.

'I made it! Be careful, Tara.'

Feeling for every contour of the rock, her friend edged slowly through the narrow crack. Head. Shoulders. *Keep going*, she thought. *The air is colder. There must be a space beyond.*

She squeezed through the fissure, and stood up straight.

'Where we are?' she gasped.

Hugh felt around with his foot. 'I'll shine the light over there, so we can... Oh!'

They had entered a vast chamber; below them was a lake, whirling, churning.

Hugh threw himself against the rock wall. 'Don't move! If we slip, we'll fall into that – that...'

They gazed in awe at the abyss, and at the night-black water.

'We're in a cathedral,' murmured Carys.

'This lake–' said Hugh. 'Where does it come from?'

'It must be the river. There are so many streams above us,' said his sister.

'This ledge could collapse...'

Suddenly, there was a gurgling noise, followed by loud drumming. They stared at the water as it began to disappear. In a few minutes, there was no lake; there were no sounds.

'What lives here?' screamed Carys, as she clung to Tara. 'A monster that drinks the water?'

'No. No. There will be a reason,' said her friend. 'Let's stay calm. We need to find a way down, cross the lake bed, and somehow get over to the other side. Perhaps there's a passage there and–'

'The waters will return, and we'll be drowned!' shouted Hugh. 'There's no way out.'

'We need to stay calm,' said Tara. 'Let's look for a way off this ledge, get down onto the lake bed, and make for those large boulders on the other side.'

She touched the bag, and ran her fingers over the Mirror. *They are terrified. What can I do? This is too much for me... too much...*

Believe... came the whisper. **Do not doubt...**

Pressing themselves flat against the wall of rock, they stood there for some minutes.

'Move the candle around, Hugh.'

'There's a track going down from this slope – but it looks slippery,' he said.

'And it's steep.'

'We can do this,' said Tara. 'Let's feel our way

slowly. I'll go first, and keep hold of your hand, Carys. Is that alright? Give us some light, Hugh.'

One by one, they slipped and slid down the wet rock path, and arrived on the cave floor.

'Ugh! Liquid mud,' muttered Tara.

Hugh moved the candle around. It flickered over some large boulders opposite.

'Shall I lead the way across to those rocks?'

'Yes. Carys and I will follow.'

Please don't let the lake return yet, prayed Tara, putting her hand on her friend's shoulder.

'Just keep going. We can slosh through this slime. It's alright. Not too deep...'

'I'm by the boulders,' called Hugh, making an arc of light. 'Come over here. A few steps more... Give me your hand...'

Carys grabbed hold of Hugh's wrist, and fell against a large slab of stone.

'I'm so frightened the lake will return. We can't go back, we can't go–' She sobbed. 'We are trapped down here – in the darkness...'

'There's this stub of candle left,' said her brother. 'And one more after that.'

Tara swallowed hard. *I must do something*, she thought.

'Do you want to wait here, while Hugh and I climb on up and see if there's a tunnel...?'

'No, no!' Carys gripped her friend's arm. 'Don't leave me here.'

Hugh had already scrambled up the boulders. He

called down, 'There's a strong draught – cold. There must be another passageway. Come on up!'

'Carys…?'

'We've come this far. Yes, I'll try.'

'Shine the light down here, Hugh, so we can see where we're going.'

Taking a deep breath, Carys stretched out her hands. 'Argh!'

'Carys – what's–?' said Tara.

'No, I'm alright.' She began to crawl up the boulder. 'Tara! It could move under me–'

'Take it slowly. Put your foot down carefully–'

'I've found a tunnel–'

'Where does it lead to?'

'I don't know. It curves and slopes down. I couldn't see the end. Come on!'

Tired and exhausted, the girls heaved themselves up the smooth boulders to the rock passage.

It was pitch-black. Were they above a gorge? Would they fall?

'Small steps. Be careful.'

'Hugh! Where are you? I can't see anything,' said Carys, stretching out her fingers in front of her. 'We need light.'

Tara stumbled on the uneven ground; she gripped her bag to her heart.

Came a whisper:

Slowly, slowly along this track,
Feel your way in this night-black.

'This is endless...' Carys hung onto Tara. 'This air... so musty...'

Hugh appeared, waving the candle.

'Come on! This tunnel curves around. And mind your heads as you go. What a sight it is up ahead! It's amazing! Wait till you see this!'

Tara lowered her head, and followed Carys along the long passage. They came out onto a platform of rock, jutting out from the cliff-face.

'Look!' said Hugh, as he swung the candle around. 'Another cavern!' Extraordinary shapes hung down from the roof. Some were short and thick; others long, thin and spiky. From the floor way below them, solid forms reached up to touch white-grey fingers.

Tara stood still. She could feel these pillars breathing.

Now they were deep inside the cliffs. Were there more chambers, more passages, further on? *Carys is right. This is endless.*

Tara steadied herself and touched the Mirror. *What shall we do? This is like a honeycomb. O Goddess. Protect us, I beg you.*

Silence. No whisper came.

Please. Don't abandon us here.

'I'm frightened,' called Carys. 'Shine the light over here, Hugh.'

At that moment, a bat flitted past and brushed his arm. Startled, he put out his hand to grip onto the walls. Wet. Slimy. Mossy.

'Argh!' he shouted. 'I'm slipping! Catch hold of me!'

Carys grabbed his arm just before he fell into the depths below. His foot caught the very edge of a narrow shelf. He clung to the cliff face with one hand.

'The candle. Take it.'

Tara reached for the candle.

'Don't let me go, Carys!'

'Try and climb back up here. Maybe there's a track.'

Keeping his face to the wall, Hugh shuffled along the slice of rock.

'I'll try.'

As he moved, some rocks crashed down, down into the void. The sounds echoed around the chamber.

'Argh!'

'Be careful!' shouted Tara.

Careful... ful... ful...

Carys suddenly noticed water bubbling up from the ground below. 'The lake! It's coming in here! Into this cavern!'

'Stay where you are, Hugh. We'll have to climb down and wade through it this time,' said Tara. 'It looks shallow enough at the moment. We'll have to go now! We have no choice.'

'But I can't–' cried Carys.

'I'll help you. Come on. We must go. Hugh, turn around slowly, feel for places to put your feet. I can see some.'

One by one, the three tentatively felt their way down.

'Not much further!'

Carys slipped and slid down the last part of the slope. 'I – I –'

'We can't stop. This is going to flood,' said Tara. 'Are there some steps in the rocks over there...? Leading up – over to the right? That might be a way out of here.'

'I can't see,' said Carys. Her whole body was trembling. 'Tara–'

'We have to cross this.'

'The water's over my ankles already!' Hugh cried out. 'It's rising so quickly. Argh!'

'Goddess. Save us!' begged Tara.

Loud drumming and the strange gurgling sounds echoed again around the walls of this cavern.

Don't panic, Tara told herself. *Because of the storms, there's a lot more water.*

'We are trapped,' yelled Hugh. 'Drowned – just like...'

Gripping the Mirror tightly Tara pleaded, 'O Goddess, we need you. I implore you...'

It was at that moment she felt a presence. Was the Goddess near? Had she come to save them?

Came the whisper:

Feed not fear
In this place of night
Breathe deeply throughout,
All will come right.

Then a soft voice.

'Guardian of the Bronze Mirror.
Hold it. Hold it high above you.
To give light, to give hope, to see all anew...'

Immediately, a rainbow appeared; an arc of colours: blue, green, yellow, red, orange. The chamber was lit up in a blaze of light; twisted pillars, terraced mushroom-like folds of rock.

'Awesome!'

'A miracle!'

'See! There are steps going up — over there, just like you said, Tara... on the right,' shouted Hugh.

'You two go first, and I'll follow.' She whispered her thanks to the Goddess.

They waded through the edge of the lake, holding onto the large boulders. Scrambling up the rock steps, they sat on a shelf high above the waters. There, huddled together, cold, wet and shivering, they listened to the gurgling and sucking noises echoing around the vast space.

Time passed; the rainbow dimmed and faded. They were now in utter darkness, each with their own thoughts.

Carys could feel a pain in her heart. Tears began to trickle down her cheeks. She remembered the last time she had seen her father. He had kissed her on the top of her head, told her to help her mother, and to take care of the family. 'We'll be back tonight,' he'd said. Then he and James had disappeared into the woods. Her throat tightened.

Sobs began to rise up, and she wanted to choke. *I'll never see them again.*

'We're going to die here,' cried Hugh. 'No one will come to save us.'

'As long as we stay calm and believe, we will get out. Don't despair. Ever.' Tara paused. 'The Goddess sent the rainbow; she sent us hope. Now, we need to breathe, in for two, hold, and out for three. Breathe like a baby. All will be well.'

They sat there in the deep night darkness for what seemed like hours.

'Shall I light the last candle?' asked Hugh.

'Better save it. We don't know how long...' began Tara.

'...we are going to be buried in here,' wept Carys.

Tara felt such grief and fear coming from her friends. *I need to support them,* she thought. *But this is so hard.*

Every so often, she suggested they sip the water that was trickling down the walls. 'As long as we drink, we can stay – er – we will be fine.'

'Sing us some songs, Hugh,' said his sister as she made an effort to keep up their spirits.

'My songs are the songs of the birds, the music of the trees. It would make me too sad.' The young boy sighed heavily.

'Shall we light the candle for a short while?'

'Yes... it will help...'

He struck the tinder box. The light flickered over a narrow slab of rock jutting out above them.

'Look! I think I saw something. Up there.'

Carys twisted her head around. 'I can't see anything.' She stood up, stretched out her hand, and felt along the ledge. 'Hold the candle higher.'

'Anything?'

'No, nothing.'

'Try again. Feel over to the right.'

She peered into the void below. 'I'll fall.'

Tara gripped her knees. 'I've got you. Don't be afraid.'

Carys reached as far to the right as she dared.

'Oh! There might be something – I'm not sure–'

Hugh waved the candle around in a circle. 'Reach further along. Something... it's square...'

'Keep hold of me, Tara.'

'Nearly got it–'

The tips of her fingers touched something. Slowly, carefully, she nudged it along.

'It's got hard sides...'

'You've nearly got it!'

'Ah – one more...' The object tipped into her hands.

Tara held her friend tightly. 'Turn around slowly, very slowly. Keep your back to the wall. Bend your knees. You won't fall. I promise.'

Carys slid down the rock face. 'It *is* a box.'

The light flickered and caught the gold on the lid. 'It is the casket!'

They gazed at the blue-and-gold box. Carys ran her fingers over the decoration.

'Beautiful.'

'It is.'

'A treasure,' whispered Hugh.

Yet none of them felt the happiness they imagined they would.

'For this, Father and James died,' said Carys. Tears streamed down her face. 'I want them back, I want Father and James back, not this golden box.'

All Tara felt was relief. The first task had been fulfilled. Or had it? Now they had to find a way out from the cave.

'Look! The water is rising higher,' shouted Hugh. 'It'll cover this rock. We can't stay here. We must go up higher.'

Tara stared at the sheer wall of rock. 'I think we should swim through it.'

'No. It's no good,' said Hugh. 'I can't swim. I'll find somewhere. I'll just wait for the tide to go out, then I'll make my way out.'

'But Hugh, will you feel safe here on your own – in the dark?'

'I'll climb up higher. There'll be a ledge and I will sit and wait there. I can sing my songs. And it'll only be for an hour – or two. Until the waters go down.'

He swallowed hard. He didn't want to stay there alone, but he knew if he tried to swim, he would drown.

'Will you be alright?'

'It's dangerous,' said Carys. 'But I'll try.'

'I promise I'll breathe properly. And drink some water.' He forced a laugh. 'That's amazing we've found the casket. Don't lose it now!'

Carys held the golden box close to her heart. Whatever happened, she was determined not to let it go. 'I'm doing this for my family, living – and dead,' she whispered.

'If we take a deep breath, we can duck down and swim straight ahead,' said Tara. 'I'll be behind you all the way.'

Carys nodded.

'Can you swim by just kicking your legs?'

'I'll try.' She turned back to her brother. 'See you soon, Hugh.'

'Yes.' He choked. 'You will.' Then, more firmly, 'I'll hold the candle high, so you can see your way down.'

Lowering themselves onto the top of the steps, the girls scrambled and slid down until they reached the water. Each had a treasure: Tara, the Bronze Mirror; Carys, the golden casket.

'We don't know what's in here,' said the young Welsh girl as they waded into the murky slime.

'The Goddess is protecting us, guiding us on our way. Soon we'll be outside in the fresh air, in the sunlight, laughing with David and Simone.'

'And Bethan.'

'And our lovely puppy. Dig deep inside, Carys. We can do this.'

The water had risen so fast, it had flooded the chamber.

The moment had come; they had to dive.

Came the whisper:

Do not falter,
For this world you must alter...

Carys closed her eyes, took a deep breath, and launched herself into the water. In a second, she had disappeared beneath the surface. Tara counted to fifty, held the Mirror tightly to her heart, and dived in head-first. Immediately, her nose began to fill with the salty water. Down her throat and into her mouth it trickled.

Dirty. Filthy. I need to breathe, she thought. *But I mustn't.* She dived deeper, kicking her legs, swimming forwards.

Time slowed: seconds, a minute, then two, passed. *I'm struggling.* She kicked again, to move through the dark, sludgy waters. *Being dragged down... my tunic... wool... so heavy... so very heavy...* Her fingers began to loosen on the Mirror.

Something, someone, caught her around the waist; she was thrust down, deeper, deeper, then along, and up, up, towards the surface. She touched something soft and wet – Carys's tunic! She let go, kicked again, and struggled forward. As her feet hit stones, she lifted her head. Air! Coughing and choking, she splashed through the waters towards the light.

Carys lay on the sandy bank, panting, but still

clutching the casket.

Flinging herself next to her friend, Tara rolled over and stared up at the rock ceiling. 'We did it!' she shouted. 'We did it!'

Carys spat out some water. 'Simone wouldn't have – liked that!'

They looked at each other, and burst out laughing.

'Look at us!'

'Dirty, slimy–'

'–filthy, muddy!'

'But – we found the casket!' said Carys.

'And we're alive!'

Picking themselves up, they staggered out of the cave.

'David! Simone! Are you there?' Tara wiped the mud off her face with her sleeve. 'We're back! Carys and I – we're here!'

Bethan raced up to them, sniffed, then sat. She put her head on one side, and whined.

'I know, puppy. We really stink!' Tara grinned and patted Bethan's head.

David called, 'Are you OK, Twin?'

'Yes – just about! Beware! We're just a bit muddy!'

The two girls blinked and shielded their eyes as they came out of the entrance.

'Here it is – the treasure – the casket,' said Carys.

'Awesome!'

'Hugh is following when the tide goes out,' said Tara. She stretched out on the grassy bank. 'Phew!'

Her friend sank to the ground, and handed the golden box to Simone. 'Take it. See – peacock. On lid. Gold.'

'*Magnifico!*'

'Oh!' said Simone, wriggling her nose. 'You two do smell!'

☆☆
☆ Chapter 14
The Treasure

Hugh had been staring at the water level for what seemed like hours. It was difficult to see if it had gone down. He had tried making up songs about bats and otters, but nothing was happening. *I need to be in the sunlight. I am a bard. If I get out of here, I'll wander the country, singing my songs. Carys is right, for me to be a soldier is a terrible idea. She loves making pottery, tiles with different patterns – and bowls, too. She can teach Meghan and Liam.*

He was talking when something touched his head. 'Ergh! Bats, spiders. I'll be glad when I'm home.' He brushed it off. The light flickered and died. 'Oh no! I'll have to crawl inch by inch out of this cave in the pitch-dark...'

Just then, a hand caught hold of his shoulder. Fingers touched his face. The boy froze. A monster! There was total silence. Hugh began to tremble. He could not breathe. He tried to move his arm away, but it was held in a tight grip. Inky blackness surrounded him; he felt eyes boring into the back of his head.

Maybe it's a ghost. I could talk to it. Beg it to let me go. He felt rising panic. *I need to be brave.* 'Where – er – who – er – why are you here?' he stuttered.

There was a strangled cough. Minutes passed. The young boy tried to think of something to say. 'Have you – have you been here for a long time?'

A groan echoed around the cavern, and Hugh's shoulder was released. He shuffled further away from the sound.

I could crawl down this ledge, wade through the water – it must have gone down by now – and be free, thought Hugh. *The others have got out. I only need to feel my way–*

A voice, croaky but clear, came from above him. 'Stay – stay with me.'

'Oh, it's fantastic to see the sun and sky!' said Tara, stretching her arms out wide as she skipped along the riverbank.

'And your twin and cousin! And Bethan, too!' David added, as the puppy wagged her tail furiously.

'So – you found it!' Simone held up the blue-and-gold casket. '*Bellissimo!* Isn't it beautiful?' She turned it around, to examine the decoration. 'How it glitters!'

'You can see the peacock clearly,' said David.

'I've seen one like this. It was in–' She was passing the casket to David when a tall young boy, dressed in livery, appeared from behind a clump of trees. 'I'll take that.'

'Tristran!' exclaimed David, as the box was snatched from his hands.

'This doesn't belong to you,' said the squire, holding it behind his back.

'It doesn't belong to you, either.'

'I will take it to Lord John. I heard from all your talk that it is his casket.' He sneered. 'You should have taken better notice when you were in the Priory. And in the Abbey. Even your dog didn't notice me!'

He was turning to walk away when Bethan growled and started barking. She crouched down and bared her teeth.

'Get that animal away from me,' shouted the boy, backing away. He aimed a kick at her head.

The spaniel leapt up and bit his arm.

'Argh! I'll beat it!' Tristran tried to push her away. 'Tell it to stop. Oh, my arm! You beast!' He staggered backwards, towards the river.

No one knew quite how it happened, but he seemed to trip as he was trying to get away from the puppy. The casket flew out of his hands. Up and up it spun, it whirled, and, as it started to fall, Simone raced to catch it before it fell into the fast-flowing waters.

The would-be knight made a grab for it, but overbalanced, crashing backwards, down the muddied riverbank, and into the torrent.

'Help! Help!' cried Tristran. 'Save me!'

Carys and David ran to get some branches for him to hang onto, but the current had already caught the boy and carried him down river; he disappeared below the surface.

'His clothes will surely pull him down,' said Carys, shaking her head, 'and there are deep pools.'

They all watched the currents swirl; the river flowed on down to the sea.

Tara held the Mirror to her heart. 'Please save this boy,' she begged.

Came the whisper:

Cunning and guile,
Deceit and greed;
Desiring treasure
To disaster leads.

They sat on the bank, in silence and in shock.

'I know he shouldn't have followed us, and he tried to take the casket, but I wouldn't have wished this on my worst enemy. And I think he probably was,' David said, shaking his head. 'He thought he was my foe. But I didn't see him like that.' He pulled at some tufts of grass. Bethan nuzzled him.

'I wish this hadn't happened.'

His cousin opened her mouth to speak.

'And please don't say it's the curse of the casket,' he said crossly. 'He was a bully and a boaster, but in time he may have learnt.'

'I wasn't going to say that, David.' Simone hunched her shoulders and folded her arms.

'Well – what were you–'

'*Bore da!* Good morning to you all!'

A monk in black-and-white robes shouted to them across the river.

Bethan jumped up, and began barking at him. 'Shush! We've heard enough from you today.' The puppy settled down at David's feet, and put her head on her paws.

Carys quickly hid the casket under some branches, and covered it with a pile of twigs.

'Who's that?' whispered Tara.

'Brother Mark, from the Abbey,' said Carys.

The monk's voice carried across the water. 'I found a young boy clinging to a branch further down the river. He said he knew you. I'm taking him to the infirmary.'

The children exchanged glances and sighed in relief.

'But he might tell them what we've found,' murmured Carys.

'He's got a fever,' the monk continued, 'babbling on about mirrors and treasure, boxes and being a knight. It'll be a while before you'll see him again.

Be careful of that cave.' He chuckled. 'It's full of ghosts! People go in and never come out! Well – I'll take my leave of you.'

Brother Mark turned, walked into the woods, and disappeared.

'Thank you for saving Tristran,' said Tara, touching the Mirror.

'And let's hope no one believes his stories when he starts ranting again,' said David. 'See, no curse!' He grinned at his cousin.

Simone turned away, frowning. 'Shall we open the casket now, or wait for Hugh?' she asked the girls. *I'll ignore him*, she thought. *He can be so, so annoying.*

They sat in a circle, and stared at the precious box. Carys glanced at the river. It was still high. 'He might be some hours yet.'

'Shall we vote?' asked David.

'What's vote?'

'We each put up our hand if we agree with something. If we don't agree, then we don't put up our hand. The most votes wins.'

'Can I do that?' asked Carys.

'Yes, of course,' said the time-travellers all at once. 'We are all equal,' added David. 'Except my twin, who was born twenty minutes before me, and is much smarter than I am!'

'He's so right!' laughed Tara.

'I propose we open this casket,' said David. 'Hands up.'

'Cool. Everyone agrees. Bethan, too!' He lifted up her paw.

'This is good,' said Carys. 'Do you always vote on things?'

'Except when our parents decide things for us,' sighed Simone.

'But they always ask for our opinions,' David said hurriedly.

Carys was turning the casket this way and that. 'Do we need a key?'

'Try putting your fingernails underneath the lid, wriggle them around, and see if it lifts up,' said Tara.

'It might be a bit stiff, from being in the cave for so long,' said her twin. 'Was it wet in there?'

'Cold, chilly, damp.'

'Freezing, smelly, and full of bats.'

'*O Dio mio!* You are brave.'

What do you think is in here, Twin? David mind-messaged Tara as Carys was trying to open the box.

I really don't know.

Carys was struggling with the catch when the lid flew open.

Tara touched the Mirror. Came the whisper:

For silver and rings,
For gems and gold,
Was it for this
You were so bold?

The four peered inside the golden casket.

'Oh, I didn't expect that!' exclaimed Simone.

'Neither did I,' said David. 'There's no silver, no jewellery…?'

'A parchment!' Tara smiled. 'You're needed again, cuz. Something for you to translate.'

'What would we do without you?' grinned David.

Simone was unrolling the roll of vellum when Carys exclaimed, 'There's something else in here! Wrapped in silk.'

'Show us, then!' said David.

Carefully, she lifted the object out of the casket, and placed it on the ground. As she uncovered it, she gasped, 'Oh, so beautiful!'

'What is it, Carys?' asked Tara.

'I hadn't imagined anything like this.'

Simone looked up from reading the scroll. 'What is it?'

Putting both hands around it, the young Welsh girl lifted it to the sky. It shimmered, sparkled, and dazzled, reflecting the rays of the sun, the drifting clouds, the waters of the Wye.

'A pure quartz vase,' whispered Tara. 'Rock crystal. Ice created by the gods and goddesses, from the beginning of time.'

'Bellissimo!'

'Cosmic!'

'Where did it come from? Who put it there? Edward?' asked Carys.

'Perhaps the answers are in the scroll,' said Tara.

'I need a few minutes,' said Simone. 'This Arabic is difficult to translate.'

The others continued to admire the crystal vase. It sparkled milky-white, rose, and hues of blue and green.

'It must be rare,' said Tara. 'I wonder where it comes from?'

'But what are we going to do with it?' asked Carys. 'I imagined the casket would be full of gold and silver from Lord John's palace. I believed Edward had stolen precious gems, and hidden them in there. Father and James risked their lives for this – this vase? I thought we had come here to... to...' She stopped. 'If there had been jewels, we could have returned them to the Lord, and received some benefit. Perhaps our lands would be ours again.'

She stared at up at the cliffs. An eagle soared way above the tree line.

'Why did you come? For this? It doesn't seem worthwhile. Any of it.'

She wiped away tears, as thoughts of her father and brother crowded in.

'You will get your land back. Lady Katherine will ask Lord John, and all will be well. Your *quitclaim* will be granted.' Tara put her arm around her friend. 'This has all been for a reason. Sometimes we don't know why things happen. Never give up. Hardships always make us stronger.'

'There have been so many,' sighed Carys. 'So many.'

Tara mind-messaged her twin. *Time to change the vibes.*

'Now, what are we going to do with this vessel – this glass vase thing?' asked David. 'And the casket – well, it has to be rare.'

Simone was examining the document. 'It is. It's from Limoges. I saw one like it in Paris, when I went with my parents. This says that the vase is from Egypt.' She turned to her cousins. 'This amazing! You know my father is from Egypt, from Cairo. This was created there, in the time of the Fatimids, in 1036.' She pointed to the vase. 'See – it has a name on it – Caliph al-Zahir. And there's a crescent moon.'

'What a find! It's a thousand years old!' exclaimed David. 'Cool!'

Carys looked confused, 'You mean over three hundred and fifty years old.'

David grinned at his twin. 'Must practise my numbers!'

Simone was reading aloud. '"Drink from this and you will never be thirsty." I think that's what it says. It protects and shines a light to all. This – this is a precious vase. It was sent to a king or queen of Portugal, or Aragon.' She squinted at the words. 'Or maybe somewhere in Burgundy – that's France, isn't it? Anyway, this vase is a gift, from the Caliph, the ruler of Egypt.' She paused. 'It is to have – to make – I must get this right. It says, "Whatever religion people have, whatever their beliefs, all peoples in this world can live at peace with each other."' She rolled up the parchment.

'There! *Benissimo!* Isn't that awesome? I must tell my parents.'

'Let's wrap it carefully in the silk again, to keep it safe,' said Tara. 'It's so precious. Then we can–'

As Carys was placing the vase back in the casket, a figure covered in brown slime came stumbling out of the cave, and dropped onto the bank beside them.

'I – I–'

'Hugh!' shouted Carys. 'You are safe!'

'Are you alright?' asked David.

'Yes – yes. I am now.' He held his chest, coughed, spluttered, and spat out some filthy water.

'That cave – never – never – go in there again. Ever...'

The puppy licked his hands. 'Oh, Bethan. Good it is to see you – and heaven to be out of that darkness.'

'I'll get you some water,' said David. 'Lie there and rest.'

'*Diolch.* Thank you. I sipped some from the walls. I'll wash later. Listen. I must tell you–'

'And we have so much to tell you–' began Simone. 'We nearly lost the casket because a boy – Tristran – tried to steal it, but then he didn't. David knows him. He'd been following us since we left the castle, but we didn't hear or see him. Then Bethan jumped up and bit him, and he fell in the river, and we thought he had drowned, but the monk saved him–'

Hugh looked at her in bewilderment.

'Don't worry. The casket is safe.' David said. 'We've just opened it because we didn't know how long you'd be. It's not exactly what we thought–'

'It's amazing! It's a rock quartz vase from–' said Tara, but stopped as a tall, thin figure emerged from the cave entrance.

Carys put her hand to her mouth. 'Oh! Oh!'

Who's this? David mind-messaged his twin. *Has someone else come to steal the casket? Has everything been a lie? Is this Edward?*

Tara replied. *Here's the treasure we came to find.* She smiled and walked towards the figure, who was covering his eyes. 'James?'

The young man nodded once, staggered, and collapsed on the ground. His tunic was ripped; his body was covered in mud. 'Let me rest here. Just for a while.'

Chapter 15
Return to the Stones

Later that day, they were all sitting outside the cottage at the top of the valley. Some fishermen had seen them on the riverbank, and taken them across the river. Rhiannon's husband was passing by with his cart, and had given them a lift.

All were so amazed at James being discovered that no one inquired as to how it had happened, or why the children had gone into the cave. 'We just had a feeling,' said Carys.

She had helped her elder brother climb slowly and painfully down from the cart. Then Eva had hugged her son tightly, while Meghan and Liam ran around laughing, clapping their hands, and shouting, 'James! James!' Bethan joined in too, shaking mud all over everyone, rolling on her back, and waving her paws in the air.

'What would we do without you, little puppy?' Simone laughed as she tickled her tummy. The twins exchanged glances. Was their cousin chilling out?

'A miracle!' cried Eva. 'My boy has come back! Returned from the dead. Come inside and lie down. Rest. Fetch some water, Liam. The special water from St Anne's Well.' She smiled at her daughter. 'I've recovered. Now I can care for James. You have all done a great deed. *Diolch. Diolch.* We must go on a pilgrimage to St David's, and give thanks.'

The children lay on the ground, exhausted. The spaniel laid her head in Hugh's lap.

'I'm sorry that it wasn't totally good news for you,' said David.

'To have found James is truly a miracle,' said Hugh. 'We thought when Father's body was discovered by the weir that our brother had been swept out to sea, that we would never find him.' He added, 'Our treasure is our brother.'

'All we need now is for–' started David.

Loud trumpeting could be heard in the forest. Shouting. Calling. Horses' hooves stamping and coming nearer. Birds flew up from the trees. Rabbits scurried through the undergrowth.

A tall, fair-haired woman, dressed in a gown of dark red and a light veil, entered the clearing. The children scrambled to their feet. She glanced at the cottage, noted the few sheep and pigs, then asked, 'Which of you is Carys ap Morgan?'

The young girl put her shoulders back and stepped forward.

'I am Carys.'

'My mistress, Lady Katherine, wishes you to have this.' She pulled out a document from a blue silk bag. 'This states that these lands belong to your family in perpetuity, by order of John of Gaunt, Lord of the Marches. Your *quitclaim* has been granted.' She paused. 'Further, Lady Katherine has instructed me to give this bag to you, Carys ap Morgan. She says you are a courageous young woman, and trusts you will always be so. You were brave to stand up for truth and justice. May you and your family have a good and happy life.'

With that, the lady pressed the document and the bag into Carys's hands, turned, and vanished into the woods.

'My – our – grateful thanks to Lady Katherine,' the astonished girl called after her. 'And Lord John–'

She caught sight of a figure on horseback at the edge of the clearing, holding a goshawk. A nod of the head, and the woman and the horse were gone. Trumpeting sounds and calls filled the forest. Foxes, pheasants and hares raced for cover.

Hugh rushed up to Carys, who was standing speechless. 'We have the land back, sister.' He turned. 'I must tell Mother – and James.' He disappeared into the cottage, calling, 'All is well! We can stay here! Forever!'

Carys shook her head in wonder. 'Another miracle,' she said. 'This is too much.'

'Lady Katherine is right. You are strong and brave,' said Tara.

'And you never gave up. You deserve it,' agreed her cousin.

'What goes around comes around,' added David.

His twin started to give him The Look.

'Well – it does – do good and those deeds come back to you. Do bad things, and they definitely come back to haunt you! I know!' He turned to Carys. 'We – no, I – learnt that when we on En... Ence..., one of the moons of Jupiter, before we came down – er – here.' He stopped, feeling a very definite glare from his twin.

'That sounds like Purgatory,' smiled Carys.

'Oh, it was!' sighed David. 'Believe me!'

Meghan and Liam came running towards their sister.

'What's in the bag, Carys? Can we see?'

The young girl pulled the strings loose at the top. 'Feels like metal.' She tipped the silk bag on its side, and into her palm dropped several gold coins and a brooch.

'How kind of Lady Katherine! Now we will never be in want. And a beautiful brooch, too. I shall give it to Mother.'

'May I see it?' asked Tara.

Carys handed it to her friend.

'A swan with a deer. It's enamelled.'

'*Bellissimo!* How beautiful!'

'It was Mary de Bohun's!' exclaimed David.

'Remember – Henry Bolingbroke's wife.'

'It was in the chest in the library,' said Simone. 'Thomas the clerk had stolen it.'

'I can't keep this,' Carys said. 'There must be some mistake.'

'It is yours, sister. She gave it to you because you are brave.'

'I suppose if times are hard again, we can take this and go to the next Lord of the Marches, and request help.'

'Be careful,' said David. 'You don't want to meet another William Sargeant, or Thomas ap Pryce. They'd have it off it you as fast as – as...'

'As a stuffed dummy of a knight that swings around and around, and hits someone in the nose!' laughed Tara.

Hugh became serious. 'Perhaps we should bury the coins and the brooch in a secret place. In case war comes to these parts.'

'Good i–'

Tara frowned at her twin. She had caught his thought – that he'd come back and dig for it when they returned to the twenty-first century.

He mind-messaged his sister. *Just a passing thought...*

'Now,' she said, 'what to do with the casket and the vase?'

Carys broke in. 'We have no need of this golden box. Or the crystal vase from the East, given from a Caliph to a king or a queen. We have our precious

James, our family, our land, and enough money for our lifetimes.'

'And the brooch,' added her brother.

'Our lives are overflowing with love and abundance. We thank you from our hearts.'

Hugh nodded in agreement. 'If we kept the casket and vase, people would say we were thieves. And what would we do with them? We are simple folk.'

Simone was stunned. 'Are you saying that you don't want the casket?'

'What would we do with it?' said Carys. 'Edward stole it from Lord John. We don't take anything that isn't given to us. It wasn't freely given.'

'We could take them both back to our time,' said David.

'We'll take them to an official. It might be declared Treasure. By law, it will then belong to the Crown,' said Tara. 'The king or the queen.'

'And kept in a special place, where people can go to see the casket and the vase, and admire their beauty,' added Simone.

'This vase is a symbol of peace and friendship,' said Carys. 'There have been many wars between religions, nations and races. Perhaps this could help to heal old wounds.'

'Love, not hate,' said David.

'Always,' agreed Simone, as she thought of her parents. *I wish they'd stop fighting with each other.*

Tara smiled, and touched the Mirror. 'It's time for us to go back to the Stones. To our own home.'

'Grateful to you for everything, we are–' began the young Welsh boy, bending down and stroking Bethan's floppy ears. His eyes were full of tears.

'Stay a while longer,' pleaded Carys. 'I'll show you how to make pots.'

Tara shook her head. 'We must go. The portal is open. We don't know for how long.'

'There is so much I wanted to ask you,' sighed Carys. 'About your lives, where you live.'

'Everything is so different, it would take–'

'–forever!' David added, putting his hand over his heart: it was swirling with emotion.

Tara nodded. *I know*, she mind-messaged him. *It's hard.*

Simone threw her arms around Carys. 'I'll miss you!'

'Perhaps we'll meet again,' said Hugh.

Tara smiled, 'In the future. In the past, even. We are closely connected–' she added in her mind – *always and forever.*

'Can I ask?'

'About what, Hugh?' said Tara.

'Our Prince of Wales, Owain Glyndwr – if there is a war between him and the king – will he win? Will we be able to make our own laws one day, here in Wales? Please – ask the Mirror.'

'It's not allowed to know the future. And the answer may not be clear. But I will ask.'

She took the Mirror out of the bag.

But there was no whisper; clouds of blue-grey mists appeared, and then vanished. Tara shook her head.

'So it won't tell us anything?' asked Hugh.

'All I can say is – be very careful,' she said. 'There are turbulent times ahead. Remain true to yourself.' She paused. 'I have been told to tell you this, Hugh: You have been given a great and valuable gift.'

'Yes, James and the land–'

'The gift of music. The gift of song. You know you are a bard. That is your treasure.'

Hugh looked down, and patted the puppy.

'We will live in peace here, simply and quietly,' said Carys. 'There is too much prejudice in our world, too much division and conflict. So we will keep away from it. Won't we, Hugh?'

He nodded. 'And go to St David's? On pilgrimage?'

'We will,' she smiled at him. 'All of us, as soon as Mother and James are well enough.'

They arrived at Harold's Stones. Simone put her arms around Carys and Hugh. Tara and David joined in; all were silent, thinking of the journey they had been on together.

'May we be friends forever,' said Carys.

A breeze surrounded them, branches swayed, their arms dropped; they moved apart.

'I will hold the casket to my heart, until we arrive at our place. I promise,' Simone said to the friends they were leaving behind.

Tara waved once, and walked quickly towards the stones. All words had been said.

Bethan whimpered.

'Come on,' said David, as he gripped her leash tightly. 'We're going home,' he whispered, feeling a mixture of sadness and relief.

Carys called, 'Till we meet again.'

'*Hwyl fawr!*' said Hugh. 'Goodbye!'

Holding the Bronze Mirror, Tara placed her hand on each stone in turn. David and Bethan followed behind her.

Simone glanced back at the two figures still watching. 'Next year, same day... here...' she called. Then, brushing tears from her cheeks, she turned away.

As they walked, they heard the sound of Hugh's whistle, then Carys's voice:

We called from our hearts,
Across the heavens you heard our pleas.
We called you from our time,
And the Goddess, she agreed.

She sent you to our land
At our request,
To make this journey,
To fulfil this quest.

Now you must return
Through time, through space.
May the Goddess protect you,
Until you arrive at your place.

Our thanks go with you,
You have brought us peace,
We'll never forget you,
Though sun and moon cease.

Tara touched the Mirror once more. A sudden gust of wind; the thin veil parted. The portal widened.

Came the whisper:

Let go. Let go... The Universe holds you now...

Caught up in a cloud of dust, they were spun, whirled through space, past clusters of stars, past planets and their moons, and through spirals of time.

From above the Earth, Tara saw Trellech enveloped in a white mist. Images flashed past: stone walls of the castle; a coracle spinning; a chase through cloisters; crawling through fissures, through murky waters...

Came the whisper:

Don't look back,
Let go of the past.

It is gone.
Nor can it be changed.
This is the moment. The only moment.
Now is all there is.
Now.

Wild winds whipped all around them. She could hear snatches of a song; Simone groaning, Bethan whimpering, her twin soothing her. Another twist of the spiral; tumbling down, down through swirls of blue and white. *Our planet*, she thought as she watched soldiers in armour fighting with swords and lances; a crown snatched from a king's head; a monk with a greyhound wandering the hills, imprisoned; a young man with fiery red hair...

The wind dropped.

Tara felt grass beneath her. All was still. A blackbird sang. Magpies chattered in nearby oaks.

'I've got just one parcel to deliver to the farm. Then I must be back in the depot by three o'clock.'

A woman's voice called from a distance. A young girl answering, 'I haven't seen, them, Tabitha.'

The trio sat up and gazed around them: at the stones, at the trees, at their backpacks by the metal fence. Bethan wagged her tail, and strained at her leash.

'What's the matter?' David gently stroked her head. 'Do you want another walk? You've only just had one from the cottage with Hugh–'

They stared at one another.

They were wearing their own, normal clothes.

Simone touched her plait. She twirled the end around. 'Do you think we're back? Really back?'

Tara nodded, 'Yes, we are–'

'But maybe it's next week,' said David. 'Or we've arrived in a different year.'

'They'll ask us where we've been all this time.'

'Keep *schtum*. Listen. Say as little as possible.'

'What will we do with the casket and the vase?' asked David. 'They would look so good in my museum.'

'In the shed at the bottom of the garden!' smiled Tara.

Here they were, back in the field of Harold's Stones. But had they lost days, weeks, months?

'Remember–'

'Everything we find has to be given to–'

'–Tabitha!' and they collapsed with laughter.

'Let's go and face the music–' said David.

Picking up their backpacks, the three squeezed through the gate, and onto the road. The puppy kept tugging at the leash.

'Don't pull, Bethan! Heel! There are cars around! She's definitely got into bad habits since the fourteenth century,' grinned David.

'Shush, Twin!'

Turning into the field, they saw Toby, Rhys and Isabelle, with all the other teenagers working in the trenches; sifting soil, and cleaning bits of pottery.

'What time do you call this?' Tabitha was standing by the first trench. Bethan barked at her and growled.

'You are late.' She checked her watch.

'It's only a quarter past two,' said Ruth, and smiled at them. 'Did you give the puppy a good walk?'

'We did,' said Simone. 'And–' she began.

'You missed the most exciting find ever,' interrupted Tabitha. 'Toby here unearthed a buckle.' She smiled her flashing on/off smile at the boy. 'We think that it could be Roman, but we are going to clean it very carefully. Aren't we?'

David glanced over at the boy, who was kneeling at the edge of the trench, looking smug. They stared at each other. *Stick-out ears. And his eyes remind me of someone*, David thought. Who can it be?

'So,' announced the beaming archaeologist as she checked her clipboard. 'I am delighted to tell you all that Toby has won today's prize for the best find. Come up and collect your reward.'

The boy shook her hand, and received a copy of *The Roman Invasion of Britain*. He smirked. Everyone dutifully clapped.

'Tara,' whispered David. 'His eyes are like

Tristran's. It can't be. Can it?'

Pulling hard on the leash, the puppy growled at the boy.

'It's possible,' replied his twin. 'Stop that, Bethan. If you're a good girl, you'll have some treats when we get home.'

'You haven't managed to train that animal in the lunch hour, then?' asked Tabitha.

'No, and, she's a puppy. But – while we were away, er, having lunch and walking Bethan–' began David '–she found this – well – it's a kind of box. It was under a rock. Do you think it's important, or valuable, even?'

Simone held the golden casket out and tried not to laugh.

The short, stocky woman waddled forward and glanced at it. 'I don't expect so. It's probably a child's lunchbox left after a picnic. There'll be stale bread in it. No wonder the dog sniffed it out.'

'It's just – we think it might be made of gold,' said Simone. 'And inside–'

'Gold! A dog finds a gold box under a rock! How ridiculous is that?'

Alan strolled over to look at it, and brushed off the earth that Tara had carefully pressed around it five minutes earlier. 'Wow! This is awesome!'

'What is it?' The two other archaeologists gathered around him, while Tabitha flicked through the book with Toby. 'And here is Caerwent. It's a few miles from here, and this is the amphitheatre at Caerleon. We should join the dig there this summer–' She put on her plastered smile. 'When I was...'

'This truly is awesome,' said Alan. 'It *is* gold. Here's a peacock. It is beautifully carved. How extraordinary!'

'It looks as though it might come from France,' said Ruth as she and Alan began scrutinising it.

'I saw one like it in Paris, in the Louvre,' said Simone. 'That casket was made in Limoges.'

The archeys stared at the young girl.

'Probably in the thirteenth century,' she added.

There was a very long, deep silence.

She continued. 'I guess it could be here because John of Gaunt was in Limoges – where they were made – and when his brother, the Black Prince, ransacked the town and killed thousands of people, he took it and kept it.'

Tara broke in, 'Could you look inside? We did have a – a–'

'A peek,' finished her twin. 'Only, it looks very fragile. Do be careful.'

Alan placed the casket on the grass and lifted the lid. 'My fingers are too muddy. Ruth. There seems to be silk covering something. Can you show us what it is?'

Even Tabitha came over and peered into the casket, as the layers of silk revealed the quartz crystal vessel.

Ruth held it up high. There was an intake of breath.

'Stunning! See how it sparkles! '

'Radiant!'

'Spectacular!'

'Better than an old Roman buck–' David started until Tara prodded him in the back.

'There's one like that in the museum in Venice too,' said Simone. 'They are very rare, you know. Made in the–' she paused for effect '–the eleventh century – or thereabouts.'

There was a gasp from the group. *Yes, I will be an actor,* she thought. *I'm enjoying this.* She continued, 'I translated the document with it.'

Alan started to unroll the parchment as Ruth looked over his shoulder.

'It's in Arabic,' said Simone. 'It says the vase comes from Egypt; a gift from a Caliph to a European monarch. His intention was to have peaceful relations between nations, races and religions. At that time, it would be between Christians and Muslims, wouldn't it?' She smiled around at the group. They were all open-mouthed.

Ruth examined the vase. 'It seems to have a crescent carved into it. Magnificent!'

'Perhaps Bethan should have a certificate for finding it,' suggested David. Simone spluttered.

Tara bit her lip. 'Enough!' she whispered. 'We need to leave here.' She nudged her cousin. 'Now!'

'*Alora! Andiamo!* Let's go!' Simone announced. 'I'll be writing this up for the school magazine.' She smiled at Tabitha and waved. '*Ciao!*'

'*Ciao!*' called Isabelle, as they raced out of the field. 'See you tomorrow, Tara?'

'We'll catch up,' said her friend.

The three jumped on their bikes.

David put the puppy into Tara's basket. 'Freewheel down the hill?'

'Oh, yes! Fun!'

Past Harold's Stones they cycled, until they stopped at the top of the Angidy Valley. There they sat on the grass, and rolled around, laughing.

Bethan tried to lick Tara's face. 'Ergh! No! Not a good girl! Stop!'

'Wasn't that just so cool?'

'Ready for the roller coaster. Simone?'

'*Si!* Yes!

'By the way, cuz...'

'What now?

'You need a shower!' He hurtled down the hill and waved to the old lady in the garden of Awkward Hill House.

'You're back early!' said Suzi, as they raced through the front door.

'Hi, Mum. Oh, we are so hungry,' said Tara.

'Famished,' agreed David.

'There's only some of the lentil bake left over

from last night. We'll be cooking dinner later.'

'Lentil bake – yes, please,' said Simone.

The twins exchanged glances. Their cousin was changing!

'Was it fun?'

'Yes, it was! But I don't think I would've liked to have lived much longer in the fourteenth century,' said Simone, as her uncle came into the kitchen.

'Did anyone find anything?' asked Ben.

'A boy found a Roman buckle–' said Tara.

'I've got some counterfeit coins from 1398–' began David. He filled Bethan's bowl with water.

'You didn't tell us about those,' said his twin, frowning.

'And best of all,' said Simone, 'we found a casket with a vase in it.'

'That's amazing! Well done!' her aunt exclaimed.

'But we had to give it to the archeys,' said David. 'It's the property of the Crown.'

'That's terrific! So it'll be in a museum,' said Ben.

'Monmouth? Abergavenny? Chepstow?' asked Suzi.

'The British Museum,' said Simone. 'Because–'

Ben and Suzi grinned and exchanged looks. 'Or Cardiff,' said Tara hurriedly, not wanting her parents to ask too many questions.

'I forgot,' said her mother. 'Nanny Lita messaged, and wants you to stay for a few days with her and Grandpa. They've been missing you. Perhaps we'll drop you off there at the weekend.'

'Welsh cakes!' said Tara.

'And bara brith!' added David.

'You only ever think of food!' said his mother.

'And we've decided on the name for our new home. It's "The Dreaming Otter". What do you think?'

'*Si!*'

'Love it!'

'Perfect!'

The twins and Simone took Bethan for a long walk along the riverbank, and sat down in a meadow full of purple and white flowers. The puppy wandered off, sniffing excitedly at all the different scents.

'What I don't understand,' said David, lying back and staring at the sky, 'is what Edward was doing with the vase.'

'He kept that a secret, didn't he?' said Simone. 'We all thought that there would be jewels in the casket.'

'And then this beautiful, amazing rock quartz vase appeared.'

'I'm not sure he knew,' said Tara.

'Maybe he just took the box and never looked inside,' said Simone.

'No... He must have... Er – Twin. Couldn't you ask the Mirror? It is the past.'

'*Alora!* We completed the task.'

'It'd be – like a reward.'

Tara sighed. 'I'll ask.' She opened the bag, and took out the Bronze Mirror.

Spirals, swirls of grey-white mists, appeared, then a knight in black armour. He was being carried on a litter by soldiers, into a town.

Men, women and children were shouting and screaming for mercy.

'Kill them all!' The knight was waving his hand towards them. 'Kill them all!'

The soldiers were taking their swords out of their scabbards. They moved forwards.

'I can't watch this,' said Simone. 'It is terrible.'

The Black Prince, brother to John of Gaunt,
Slaughtered these people of Limoges,
His soldiers, his knights, set the town ablaze,
Stole the vessel of peace and to all brought woe.

The mists swirled once more. The images vanished.

'So when the Black Prince died, the casket was passed to his younger brother. That was Lord John. Then Edward stole it from his palace, before it burnt down.'

'It's good the vase will go to a museum,' said David. 'People can look at it, and know that hundreds of years ago, people were striving for peace. Peace between religions...'

'Peace between nations...'

'And races.'

Just then, teenagers in two canoes appeared around the bend of the river, making towards Bigsweir. As the waters carried them past, they called out. 'Hey, you guys!'

'Looks like fun!' called Tara.

'Look out for rocks!' shouted David.

Bethan bounded along the path, and threw herself on top of David.

'Remember when we nearly lost you!' he said, fussing her. 'And what happened to John of Gaunt?'

'You could find out yourself! Lazy!'

'You know you want to tell me!' smiled her twin. 'You were reading all about it after we got back!'

Tara lay on the grass and looked up at the cloudless sky. 'In a nutshell–'

'He went nuts?' Simone frowned.

'No, I'm trying to make it short. OK. Lord John died a few months after we saw him. His son, Henry Bolingbroke, was sent into exile by King Richard. Then he returned from France and fought the king. Henry won, put Richard–'

'Richard II?' asked David.

'Yes. Henry put him in prison, and he died there. He had himself crowned Henry IV. There were bad omens at his coronation...'

'So many Henrys,' muttered Simone.

'So his son was Henry V? Henry of Monmouth.'

'Exactly. And he used Welsh archers to win the battle of Agincourt. Their names can be seen in Brecon Cathedral.'

'Cool. I'd like to go there. Maybe this summer.'

'Are there–?'

'Shops? Yes!'

'So – what happened to Owain Glyndwr?' asked David.

'For fourteen years, he fought against the English kings – Henry IV and Henry V. He lost. But he was never betrayed, and no one knows what happened in the end. Some think he lived with a daughter, over the border in Herefordshire, until he died.'

'Faded away...' murmured David.

'To return, say the bards, when Wales needs him most.'

Each thought about their friends, and what may have happened to them during those years.

'I hope they went on their pilgrimage to St Davids,' said Simone.

'Hugh taught me this song when we were in the coracle going down this river. Shall I sing it?'

'With your voice?'

'It's not that bad, Twin!'

'Blow the wind over the mountains,
Blow the wind over the seas,
May it bring peace to our country,
May we always be free.'

'We've got one more thing to do,' said Tara

quickly as they were all feeling sad. 'Before we came down here, to this planet, we were given crystals, by the Goddess.'

'One task, one crystal,' said David. 'And we've completed the first one.'

'A crystal must be cast into waters,' said Tara, 'to cleanse them.'

'But we haven't got one,' said Simone. 'What are we going to do? Do we have to go back?'

Tara opened her hand. In her palm was a long, arrow-shaped crystal. 'There was a crystal inside the vase. It was placed in there for us, to do what we must do.'

'Galactic!'

She held it up to the sun. It glowed; it sparkled; golden lights radiated from it.

'May all the waters of our planet be cleansed,' said Tara, as she held the pure crystal to her heart. 'The streams, the rivers, the seas. May all be pristine once more.'

With great care, she passed the precious crystal to her cousin. 'Would you like to cast it into our river – the Wye?'

Simone held the crystal, took a step forward, and threw it high, high up into the cloudless sky. For a second, it hung there, shimmering, sparkling. Then, as it dropped into the swirling waters, the river claimed it, carrying it out to the seas, out to the oceans.